ASCENT

(THE INVASION CHRONICLES -- BOOK 3)

MORGAN RICE

ISBN: 978-1-64029-492-9

CHAPTER ONE

Kevin stared up in horror at the small ship dragging him and Chloe inside it, feeling completely helpless as it lifted them up with its beam of light. They dangled in the air, turning over helplessly as it drew them up.

It had seemed so certain that they would be able to stop the aliens using the virus they'd taken from the tar pits, but the aliens had sent the vial back empty, almost with *contempt*.

That wasn't the worst part though. The worst part was that Luna was gone. They'd made Luna one of them, and that hurt more than Kevin had thought anything could.

Chloe screamed beside him as they rose, tumbling in air that no longer seemed to know which way was down. Kevin could hear the fear there, but also the anger.

Metal closed around them, and they tumbled together onto the floor of the small ship that had sucked them up. Kevin struggled to stand, bracing himself, half expecting to be attacked by some alien force.

Instead, he found himself standing in the middle of a large, round, white-walled room. There was a circular portal on the floor that looked as though it opened and closed like the aperture of a camera, and nothing else.

Chloe went over to one of the walls and banged a fist on it.

"Kevin, what are we going to do?"

Kevin wished he had an answer. But after everything that had happened down below, he didn't think he had answers for anything anymore.

"I don't know," he said.

Chloe hit the wall again, the thud sounding dull against the interior.

"Chloe, that won't—"

Suddenly, they were standing in thin air. The wall was now as translucent as glass, giving Kevin a clear view of Sedona falling away beneath him, and the larger ship above that they were rising up to meet.

This close, Kevin could see the door—more like a cavernous mouth—open to accept them, letting their ship into what must have been a hangar. There was a ripple of something as they passed into it, some shield or membrane that must have been there to hold its atmosphere in place.

"Incredible," Chloe said with a gasp.

Kevin had to agree. The hangar was large enough for dozens of the ships, all connecting to walkways. Their ship connected to one.

They stopped abruptly, and a section of the wall slid aside, revealing an open doorway.

Kevin and Chloe stared at each other. Why weren't they being greeted? Attacked?

"So they want us to just walk out?" Chloe asked. "Why haven't they killed us yet?"

Kevin wondered that himself.

"Maybe it's a trap," he said.

She started to cry.

Kevin put a hand on her arm. He knew how bad things could get, and he found his thoughts caught between concern for her and worries about what might be happening here. Why were they alone? Why weren't they greeted by the aliens' equivalent of police or soldiers waiting for them?

"Should we walk out?" Kevin asked. "Or stay in here?"

She looked at him.

"Neither option seems safe," she said.

Chloe stepped to the opening, to Kevin's surprise, and he followed. But suddenly she stopped, walking right into something. It was an illusion—a translucent wall that stopped her from walking but allowed her to look out.

Then their small ship starting moving again, slowly, through the massive hangar.

Kevin stepped up beside her and looked out in awe. The hangar was huge and rounded, looking as much grown as built, the walls seeming to pulse faintly with power. But other than the rows and rows of ships, the space was empty.

There were no captured people, no machines working on things, and no aliens.

"Where is everyone?" Chloe asked, echoing his thought.

Kevin didn't answer, because he was too busy looking back at Earth. Sedona sat below them, seeming so close, yet so achingly far.

"Why aren't we falling down toward it?" he wondered aloud.

Chloe frowned at him, looked around, and then shrugged. "I don't know. Maybe the gravity works differently here. I'm kind of glad we aren't, though."

Kevin was glad too, because it would have been a really long way to fall. It took him a moment to realize that it seemed to be

2

getting further with every passing moment, receding little by little, the buildings growing smaller until Kevin could no longer make them out.

"We're still moving!" he said. "We're going up into space!"

In spite of everything, in spite of the horrors that had been inflicted on the world, and the danger they were probably in, in spite of the fact that they'd failed to destroy the aliens, Kevin had to admit a part of him was excited. The idea of actually going into space was almost too incredible to believe.

"It would be cool except for *where* we're going," Chloe pointed out.

Kevin could hear the fear there, and he could even feel some of it himself. If they were heading up, then there was only one place where they could be going, and that would be a dangerous place for them both. The world ship hung above, its rocky surface punctuated by spike-like towers, but almost blank aside from that.

It was frightening, yet the thing was, it might also be their best opportunity to actually *do* something about all of this.

"I know you're afraid," Kevin said. "But there's nothing we can do to stop it. And look at the bright side: we had no way of stopping them back on Earth. Maybe up here we can."

Chloe scoffed. "How?"

Kevin shrugged. He didn't know yet. There had to be something. Maybe there would be some way to shut down the things the aliens were doing. Maybe there were ways to drive them off, or fight back against them, or even kill them.

"We have to try," Kevin said.

He couldn't help thinking about Luna. What had happened to her was a lot worse than being transported in some alien ship.

They stood there quietly, watching as the Earth grew smaller and smaller beneath them. Soon, it was the size of a watermelon, then a baseball, then a marble against the night sky.

Kevin turned and looked at the mother ship. He hadn't realized quite how big the alien world was before, and it was only as the craft turned and shifted in space that he got a real sense of how large it was.

"It's an actual world," Kevin said, unable to keep the awe out of his voice.

"We knew that," Chloe said. "It's been up in the sky."

"But an actual *world*…"

There was a big difference between seeing something far off and being there. Like the moon, Kevin could have covered up the world ship with the palm of his hand from Earth, but now that they

3

were here, it stretched out as far as he could see in every direction. There were structures on the surface, although most of it looked barren and empty, with only giant towers sticking up from it like the spines of a sea urchin. There were also mouthlike apertures, big enough that even a ship like the one they were on could fit into them without touching the sides. Kevin couldn't imagine what might have carved gaps like that into a world, but right then they had bigger things to think about.

"I think we're going into it," Kevin said. Not just to a world, but inside it, down past the outer shell of its surface.

Chloe didn't look happy about that. "We're going to be trapped. We'll never find our way out."

"We will," Kevin reassured her.

He had to believe that. The alternative was that they were heading down to their deaths as the ship that carried them descended into the surface of the world…

…and through it.

Kevin stared. The entire interior of the world ship was like a hollow shell, and inside it there was everything Kevin might have expected on the surface of a planet. There were oceans and landmasses, vehicles moving back and forth, and cities so huge they seemed to take up almost every scrap of available land, turning the whole great ship into one giant hive of activity. Spires stood out from different spots on the vast city, golden and gleaming, looking like palaces set against the rest. A great reddish-gold orb pulsed at the heart of the planet, giving off heat and light.

Kevin thought he could see figures down below, but they were too distant to make out the details yet.

"Aliens," Chloe said, staring down. "Not people controlled by them, not messages, not their voices… aliens."

Kevin knew what she meant. All this time, they'd had only hints of the aliens, seen only the effects of what they could do. Now, here they were on the aliens' world, and there was so *much* of it.

They felt the clunk as the ship that carried them locked into place on the world, steadying their view of a city beyond in which creatures of every impossible shape and size walked at strange angles, seemingly held in place sideways and upside down in defiance of gravity, or maybe they just had control of the gravity, so that any direction could be "down."

This time, the door opened for real. Kevin could feel the slight breeze on his face, warm and balmy, smelling unlike anything he'd ever experienced.

4

What surprised him the most, though, was what lay waiting on the other side.

A trio of figures stood there, waiting to greet them.

They were almost identical, which in this place seemed like an impossibility to Kevin. They were tall and hairless, pale-skinned, with eyes that reminded Kevin of a wasp's, except that they were a pure, milky white. They wore long robes over pale jumpsuits, and each seemed to have an assortment of metal, and occasionally fleshy, devices set around its body.

The one standing at the heart of the trio spoke. Its words came out in English from a translator on its arm, but Kevin didn't need it to translate the flat monotone. His brain did that for him.

"Welcome, Kevin McKenzie. We have been waiting for you."

CHAPTER TWO

Kevin stared at the alien who had spoken, horror flooding through him.

The alien stared back at him with those large pale eyes, and it spoke again while the two others beside it stood silent, the words translating in Kevin's head before the device it held could do it.

"This one is Purest Xan of the Hive," the alien said. "The two beside this one are Purest Ix and Purest Ull. And you are Chloe Baxter and Kevin McKenzie, ape things of the planet Earth."

Kevin was stunned. It took him several moments to collect his thoughts.

"We're humans," Kevin said, wanting to correct them, to talk to them, even to persuade them. After all, they were talking to him in a way that they hadn't bothered talking to anybody else.

"As I said," Purest Xan replied, "ape things. Lesser things, but perhaps things worth learning from."

There was no emotion to the way the alien said it, but there was something about the way it talked about learning from them that sent a shiver down Kevin's spine.

"What do you mean?" Kevin demanded. "What are you going to do to us?"

"Our world ships travel to gather resources," Purest Xan said. "Technology, minerals, minds, bodies we can reshape. We will test you and understand you until you prove worthless. Then we will discard you."

Kevin saw Chloe's face turn pale, and he could share that fear. The thought of being ripped apart for study and then discarded was terrifying.

"We aren't afraid of you," Chloe said, struggling to put a defiant note in her voice.

"Yes, you are," Purest Xan said. "You are a lesser being, with fears and needs, weaknesses and flaws. You are not of the Hive. You are not of the Purest. We have no such weaknesses, only the improvements of our flesh shapers."

"You think you're perfect?" Chloe demanded. "You think looking like *that*, you're perfect?"

"Not yet," Purest Xan said. "But we will be. Enough speaking to lesser orders."

6

The alien turned to the others with it, and Kevin knew that the next thing it would say was *grab them*.

"Run!" he yelled to Chloe, and they spun away from the aliens, starting to sprint as fast as they could from the square. Kevin ran as hard as his body would let him, ignoring the pain and effort, ignoring the way his illness tried to drag him down with every step and hoping that, if he and Chloe could make enough ground, they might be able to lose Purest Xan and the others with it in the chaos of the world ship.

"Where are we going?" Chloe demanded.

"I don't know," Kevin said. He had no plan right then, no idea what they were going to do next.

He kept running, risking a quick look back to see if the aliens were chasing them. They just stood there, apparently concentrating. One of them touched something on its arm.

Without warning, the world felt heavier. It felt as though heavy weights were pressing down on top of Kevin, too solid to lift. He struggled to keep standing, and saw Chloe doing the same, pushing up against it as if she could lift the sky above her. It wasn't the air, though; it felt as though Kevin's own bones and muscles were too heavy, gravity dragging him down toward the floor many times harder than it should have.

"It's the stuff that lets them stick to the walls," Kevin called out, thinking of the way the aliens had been able to walk sideways and upside down through the interior of their world ship. If they could control gravity well enough to do that, of *course* they would.

Chloe shouted back, "It's dragging me down. We're *trapped*!"

She sounded on the verge of panic, just as she'd been back in the spaceship.

The gravity pulled him down to his knees, the pressure making it hard to breathe. He fell forward, feeling the weight of his own body pinning him down to the floor.

A scream of frustration from Chloe told him that the same thing must have happened to her. It took everything Kevin had just to be able to roll over onto his back and look across to where she lay, pinned in the same way.

"No, let me go! Let me *go*!" she screamed. Kevin could see her crying as she tried to thrash her way clear of the force holding her in place.

The three aliens were there then, and they must have sent some signal to others, because two hulking creatures with carapaces like armor walked out from the golden spire carrying what looked like two large metal frames. They set them down near Kevin and Chloe,

7

standing them upright so that Kevin could see the glasslike sheets set inside them, making them look like two windows standing up on their own.

"Attempting to run was foolish," Purest Xan said. The alien gave a signal to the two armored creatures, and they reached down to grab Chloe from the floor. As soon as they lifted her, she started to thrash and twist, struggling to get free, but they held her as easily as a feather while she cried.

"Stop it," Kevin said. "Leave her alone!"

It didn't seem to make any difference to them. The creatures were as implacable as machines, moving with the kind of strength that said they could have easily torn Chloe and Kevin apart. They took Chloe and lifted her against one of the clear plates, and one of the Purest pressed something on its arm again. Chloe stuck to it as surely as if they'd glued her there, still fighting against it, and still crying when nothing happened.

They came for Kevin then, and big hands clamped around Kevin's arms, lifting him and pressing him against the second glass panel without giving him any chance to fight. Kevin kicked at them, but his foot just bounced off their armored hides. Then the alien with the device touched it, and Kevin was stuck to the glass just like Chloe.

It didn't feel like being glued to something, though. There was no stickiness to it. It was more like lying down, except that he couldn't hope to get up because of the gravity pressing him into place. It wasn't as strong as on the floor; it was even quite comfortable if he didn't try to fight it, but Kevin couldn't hope to pull his way clear of it.

"Kevin," Chloe said, looking absolutely distraught as she hung there on her own frame.

"I'm right here, Chloe," he said. He didn't try to promise her that it would all be okay. That didn't feel like a promise he could make then. "I'm not going anywhere."

It turned out that they were both going *somewhere* though, because the large, armored aliens lifted the frames, carrying them like builders moving panes of glass into position. Weirdly, Kevin had no sensation of being lifted, because for him, *down* still felt as though it was toward the frame.

"Where are you taking us?" Chloe demanded. "Let us go!"

"Try to stay calm," Kevin said, hoping that none of the fear he felt in that moment crept into his voice. He was afraid of what might happen to both of them, but he was really afraid for Chloe.

With how much she hated being trapped, this was the worst possible thing that could happen to them.

Except that it wasn't, and Kevin knew it. There were still plenty of worse things that could happen. *Would* happen, if they didn't figure out a way out of it.

The aliens carried them toward a golden spire, through a large door that opened automatically to admit them. The interior was everything that the rest of the world ship was not: clean and bright and comfortable looking, so that to Kevin it looked like a very expensive hotel might have, or perhaps a palace. There wasn't the huge variety of different angles and directions here, either; unlike the rest of the ship, everyone seemed to have agreed on which way was up.

They carried Kevin and Chloe up to a room where dome-shaped banks of machinery stood, looking half-built, half-grown. A section of the wall flickered with an image of the Earth below, and Kevin didn't know if that had been done simply to stop the walls from being featureless, or as a kind of additional cruelty.

Purest Xan followed them into the room, standing between them, by one of the dome-shaped devices. It took tiny, squid-like things from an opening within the dome one by one, each no bigger than the tip of the alien's finger. Purest Xan placed them on Kevin's head, where they stuck, feeling warm and slimy all at once.

"What is all this?" Kevin demanded. "What are you doing to us?"

"We are going to examine you," Purest Xan replied. "We will see what use you are to the Hive. There will be pain."

It said it as though it was nothing, or at least as though it didn't care. Kevin could hear Chloe crying again now, and he wanted to say something, wanted to comfort her. Then the pain hit, and there was no time to do anything but cry out with it.

It felt like cold fingers rummaging around in his thoughts, picking things up and putting them back again, or maybe it was the tentacles of the things stuck to Kevin's head. He tried to push them out, concentrating as hard as he could, but it made no difference; it just brought more pain.

Kevin could feel other presences now, dozens of minds, hundreds, connected in a kind of silent communion, their collective presence pressing into him and exploring every corner of his being. He heard himself scream, and he heard Chloe too, suggesting that exactly the same thing was happening to her.

Kevin saw images then, flooding into the forefront of his mind and flickering there. There were images of friends, of family, of

9

everything that had recently happened. Kevin saw images of the Survivors jumping into his mind, and he tried to think about something, anything else, so that the aliens wouldn't know where they were. He could feel their lack of interest though; it seemed to make no difference to them.

He started to see other things, the visions flickering through the rest of it, although the truth was that he couldn't tell whether they were real visions or something flowing back along the connection to the Hive's collective. The images filled his mind, blotting out the pain, the sensation of being pinned in place, even the fear of what was happening to Chloe.

He saw a planet floating in space, huge and dull. Moons spun around it, but even as Kevin watched, he realized that they weren't natural moons, but more world ships. He saw one move out of orbit, the space around it bending and shifting as it moved impossibly fast for something that size.

He felt his consciousness being pulled down toward the surface of the planet, and as he reached it, he saw that the surface was blasted and ruined, polluted and inhospitable. There were towns there in spite of that, filled with hunched figures who looked similar to the Purest, but hunched over and changed, their flesh twisted to live in the ruined environment. Kevin found it hard to believe that anyone would want to live in a place like that, but through the connection to the Hive he knew that these figures didn't get a choice. They were the ones not chosen for the world ship.

He saw other things there. He saw the camps of creatures stolen from world after world. He saw the flesh factories where they were tested and reshaped, tortured in way after way, with electricity and fire and more. He saw creatures dissected while alive, or forced to breed with one another in combinations that produced monsters. Among the desolation of the wasted planet, he saw small green domes too, like islands of perfection among the horror of the rest of it. Kevin wasn't surprised to see golden towers standing at the heart of each one.

He came back to himself, gasping, feeling as though every scrap of energy had been pulled out of him. Kevin lay on the platform, looking around and seeing only Chloe in the room now. It felt as though the visions had only lasted seconds, but it must have been longer, to give Purest Xan enough time to leave the room.

"Chloe?" Kevin said.

He heard her groan, her eyes opening as she looked over at him. They were red with crying now as she stared over at him.

"I saw... I saw..."

10

"I know," Kevin said. "I saw it too."

"They're going to kill us," Chloe said. "They're going to pull us apart to see how we work. They're going to experiment on us like some little kid pulling the wings off flies."

Kevin would have nodded if he could have pulled his head away from the frame enough to do it. That was the problem, though: they could talk about how much they needed to get out of there, they could see everything that was going to happen, but they still couldn't move. All they could do was stay there, staring at the screen in front of them, and the Earth rotating slowly upon it.

It took a second or two to realize that it was getting smaller.

It was gradual at first, the planet shrinking away a little at a time. Then it started to move faster, and faster still, receding until it was just a dot. Then it wasn't even that as the space around the world ship folded around it and it shot away through space.

Kevin stared at the screen in horror. He didn't know where they were going, or why, but whatever could persuade the aliens to move their whole world ship from the Earth, he knew that it couldn't be good for him and Chloe.

Or for Luna.

CHAPTER THREE

Luna fought. With every scrap of energy she could find, she tried to fight back against the immobility creeping through her body, making her slow, making her stop. She stood in the middle of Sedona, at the heart of a group of controlled people, and her mind screamed with the effort of trying to keep herself from becoming like them.

It felt as though her body was turning into stone, or... no, more like her limbs were going to sleep while inside she was still awake. She couldn't feel her fingertips, but she kept on fighting. She could feel herself slipping into the controlled state, though, becoming more and more of a prisoner in her own body with every passing second. It felt as though she was trapped behind glass, her personality and her ability to control herself an exhibit in some museum made from her own flesh and bones.

The world even *looked* as though she was looking through a kind of strangely filtered glass, colors shifted so that all the ones Luna expected had a milky opacity to them, and new ones crept in around the edges of her vision. Luna didn't need a mirror to know that her pupils would be a vivid white by now, and she *hated* it.

I will keep fighting, she told herself. *I won't give up. Kevin needs me.*

In spite of her determination, it was hard to ignore the fact that her arms and legs wouldn't do what she ordered them to. Luna was just standing there, the same as all the others waiting in Sedona, as still as an unused puppet, unable to do more than blink and breathe by herself.

Luna fought to do more. She focused on the smallest finger of her right hand, willing it to straighten. It seemed to move achingly slowly, but it moved. It moved! She tried to move the next finger, focusing on each joint, each muscle...

She screamed inwardly when nothing happened.

At least Kevin had gotten away. Luna had seen him make it through the ranks of the controlled and get to one of the ships. She'd seen him and Chloe sucked up into one of them too, and that made Luna worry more than anything that was happening to her.

You have to fight, she told herself again. *Kevin is stuck on an alien spaceship without you. You know he'll just get into trouble on his own, and not even the fun kind.*

Of course, Kevin wasn't on his own, but that thought didn't make things better. It wasn't that Luna hated Chloe or anything, but it was pretty obvious that she liked Kevin, and... well... so did Luna. It was weird how that was easier to admit when her mind was busy being taken over by aliens, but it was, maybe because she knew no one else would find out.

She'd tried making it obvious to him plenty of times in the past, although he never seemed to *get* it. Maybe that was a boy thing, or maybe it was just a Kevin thing, able to understand messages from across the galaxy, but not anything right in front of his face. Now he was up on an alien spaceship with Chloe, and if they weren't exactly alone together, Luna was pretty sure that aliens didn't count. Even if nothing happened, Luna still wasn't sure that Chloe was a good choice to get Kevin back safely. Yes, she'd helped save Luna on the boat, and she could hotwire a car, but that wasn't the same thing as hijacking a spaceship, and Luna didn't trust her not to panic when things went wrong.

Then things *did* go wrong, and Luna had a perfect view of it.

One moment, the aliens' world ship was hanging moon-like in the sky; the next, the sky around it rippled and flickered, as though space was a pond that someone had thrown a stone into. The world ship started to drift away, its shadow passing from the sky. There was a moment when the space it was in seemed to fold around it, and then it was gone, moving far faster than Luna could hope to follow.

For a brief moment, hope flared in her. Was it over? Kevin had gone up into the small ship above Sedona, and that had gone up to the world ship, and now both were gone. Had he found a way to end this? Had he and Chloe saved them all?

Luna tried to move her arm, hoping against hope, but nothing happened. Nothing had changed.

A bark beside her caught Luna's attention. Bobby was there, the Old English sheepdog running up to Luna and nudging against her leg in a way that might almost have knocked her over if he had done it before the controlled breathed their vapor into her. As it was, she stood as solid as stone, unmoved and unmoving, not even reacting as he moved to her hand, licking her with a big, rough tongue.

Good boy, Luna thought, and tried to say it, but she couldn't get the sounds out. She couldn't reach out to pet him either, and that just showed her how much control the aliens still had over her. Bobby nudged against her again and then ran back as if expecting her to follow, and when she didn't, he lay down and whined, looking up at her with sad eyes.

I'm sorry, Bobby, Luna thought, but she couldn't say that, either.

It wasn't the only thing she was sorry for. Around her, Luna could see the Dustside bikers standing just as still as everyone else. She could see Bear hulking over the rest of them, all of the sense of strength and command leached out of him by his transformation. She could see Cub just a little way away, the boy staring back at her blankly, where before he'd been confident and obviously interested in her.

Are you still in there? Luna wondered in the prison of her mind. Was everyone who had been transformed trapped like this? Were they sitting there behind the pure white of their pupils, horrified as the aliens controlled every movement they made? Luna didn't know whether to hope that Cub wasn't having to suffer that, or to hope that he was, because at least it would mean that he was still there, and at least there might be a chance to get him back.

What chance? Luna thought. What hope was there for any of them? No one had come back from this so far. The aliens had transformed most of the world, and the people who got transformed stayed transformed. It wasn't like liking the wrong band; it wasn't as if it simply wore off if you left it long enough.

She could hear sounds now, deep in the back of her mind. She recognized the screeches and the clicks, the static sounds and the buzzing, because she'd heard them plenty of times before when Kevin had been translating alien signals. Luna could hear this as their language, although she still had no idea what it meant.

She might not know it, but it seemed that her body did. Luna found herself starting to move, forming up with the other people there like some kind of military unit. She didn't know who was giving the orders if the main alien ship was gone. Maybe some of the aliens were down on the surface.

It didn't matter; whoever was giving the orders to her, Luna found herself obeying them. She started to march with the others, spreading out with them among the debris of Sedona, starting to lift rubble and pick through the houses.

Luna felt like she was watching it from a distance, seeing herself lifting rocks and pulling at sections of wood with her bare hands. She saw herself moving in concert with Cub and the others, picking the town clean with the thoroughness of ants cutting leaves or vultures stripping a carcass of meat.

14

She heard Bobby barking again, and he was beside her once more, yapping and running around her as if he might be able to distract her from what she was doing. He licked her hand again, then clamped his teeth down on her arm. It wasn't hard, more like the way he might have held onto a wayward puppy and pulled it back into line.

Bobby was strong, and probably weighed almost as much as her, but Luna pulled clear of him as if he wasn't there. She kept working, gathering materials and forming them into piles, sorting them as efficiently as a machine.

Luna saw cuts and scrapes appear on her arms from the effort of moving the materials, but she didn't feel them. They were as numb as if she had left them in ice for an hour, the pain insulated from her by the layers of alien control.

Luna could feel that control now as Bobby continued to bark and run around her. She could feel what it wanted her to do, and she fought it, the small part of her that was still *her* horrified by the prospect even as the rest of her picked up a rock.

No! she commanded herself. *I won't do it. I won't do this!*

She fought against the impulses with every fiber of her being, pulling back at her arm with the full strength of a will that had previously stood up to everything from parents' instructions to the raging ocean. For a moment or two, it felt as if she was even able to make her body hesitate, frozen on the brink of action. It was too much, though, like trying to hold back the weight of an avalanche with her bare hands. With an inner cry of despair, Luna felt that avalanche pour over her.

She turned and threw the rock at Bobby, crying as she did it.

He yelped, then whined as he hurried away, limping slightly on one paw. Luna saw him retreat to the edges of the buildings they were working on, lying down and watching her with a forlorn look that matched how Luna felt only too well.

But what she felt didn't matter, not in the face of the aliens' instructions. No matter how much her mind crashed against the limits of the cage that held it, the prison of her body kept working, lifting and tearing, separating resources and stacking them ready for collection even though the ship above Sedona was gone now.

She tried to count the minutes that passed, tried to keep some track of the time that was ebbing away, but there was no easy way to do it. Her body kept her eyes on the work, not on the progress of the sun, and if she got hungry or tired, she didn't feel it. In the deepest recesses of her mind, Luna understood now how the controlled were so fast and strong: they didn't care about the pain or the tiredness that would have stopped most ordinary people; where most people stopped well short of the limits of what their bodies could do, the controlled were pushed to those limits all the time by the aliens who commanded them.

Who command us, Luna corrected herself.

She didn't want to think of herself as one of them, but Luna wasn't sure how to distract herself from any of it. She couldn't shut her eyes to block it out. She couldn't stop herself from doing any of this. The most that she could do was try to grasp for memories of her life before this: sitting with Kevin on the shore of the lake when he'd told her about his illness, going to school and... and...

She latched onto a memory, thinking about one day when she'd been due to meet up with Kevin after school. They'd planned to go down to a pizza place on the corner not far from their houses. She could remember the feeling, what it had been like walking through their town, heading for a spot that had been just theirs, that no one else had known about, behind one of the wooden fences that surrounded an old house a little way along that no one had lived in for years.

Getting there meant clambering through the fork in the old tree that kept a gap clear among a stack of old junk, then running along the boards of a low roof in *just* the right pattern that her feet wouldn't fall through, all the while making sure that no one who might shout at her for being somewhere she shouldn't be saw her.

In other words, it was exactly the kind of route that Luna loved to run along. She made her way along it with the kind of speed and willingness to get muddy that would probably have made her parents sigh if they saw it. While she ran, she found herself thinking about Kevin, wondering if today would be the day when he got around to asking if he could kiss her.

Maybe he wouldn't; he could be pretty oblivious about things sometimes.

She made her way through the gardens, over toward the spot where she and Kevin were due to meet. She heard a noise from beyond the fence, and saw Kevin and a couple of other boys she hadn't seen before.

"What are you doing back here?" one asked. "Hiding away so no one can find you?"

"I'm not hiding," Kevin insisted, which Luna guessed was just about the worst thing he could have done.

"Are you saying that I'm a liar?" the boy demanded. He pushed Kevin, so that Kevin scraped back against the wall. "Are you calling me a liar?"

Luna slipped through the gap in the fence. "I am," she declared. "I'm saying that you're a liar, and a bully, and if you give me a couple of seconds, I'll probably think of plenty of other nasty things to call you too."

He spun toward her. "You'd better run. This is between me and him."

"And your friend, let's not forget that," Luna said.

"You're being smart because you think I won't hit a girl! Well—"

Luna punched him in the nose, as much because she was getting bored waiting for him to actually do something as anything else. He roared and set off running after her as Luna sprinted away.

She didn't lead him back the way she'd come, because that was *her* route, but she knew plenty of others. Just for fun, she cut across the garden where they always had their pool filled, hearing a splash as one of the boys missed his turn. From there, she scrambled up onto one of the nearby roofs, then over through the park, then across into the garden where the big, angry dog lived, taking care to only step in the spaces out of range of its chain. A snarl and a shriek of anger behind Luna told her that the second of the boys had fallen behind.

"I'll get you for this!" he yelled out.

Luna laughed. "Not unless you want to have to explain to people how I managed to punch you and get away with it."

She ran back in the direction of Kevin, who was waiting there with the confidence of someone who'd seen this game before.

"You know, I could have taken him," he said, trying to look tough.

Luna managed not to laugh. "But it's more *fun* this way. Come on, you can buy me pizza for rescuing you."

"But you didn't rescue me. I could have taken him..."

***

Luna smiled at the memory, or would have if she'd been able to move her face. She tried to think of the bully's name, because she was sure that she'd known it once. What bully though? What had she been thinking about? The fact that she couldn't remember made Luna pause in terror. She'd been thinking about it just a moment ago, and now it was gone, like... like...

Luna tried to grasp the memories, she really did. She knew that she *had* memories; a whole lifetime's worth. She had friends, and a life, and parents... she definitely had parents, so why couldn't she remember their *faces*? Maybe she didn't have parents. Maybe all of this was just some sick joke. Maybe she'd always been like this, and she was just defective somehow, feeling that she was different as a distraction from the work that the aliens needed her to...

No, Luna thought fiercely, *I'm me. I'm Luna. They transformed me, and I have real memories... somewhere.*

She wasn't sure where, though. Every time she tried to grab for what felt like the beginnings of a memory, it slipped away into a great fog of thoughts that felt as though it was consuming every part of her. Luna tried to drag herself away from that fog, but it was creeping in more and more around the edges of who she was, seeming to fill everything, carrying away small pieces of memories, of words, of personality.

Suddenly, she saw something. It was just different enough to snap her out of it, even if just for a second.

There was a man approaching. Moving forward without fear. A real man. Not controlled.

How could that be?

Where Luna and the others moved with an almost mechanical synchronization, he moved forward in furtive little darts and stutters, with what looked like some kind of gun cradled in his arms.

He didn't look like a soldier, though. He looked more like a pirate, crossed with a professor. His hair was wild and spiked, while half a dozen earrings dotted one ear, and he had the beginnings of an unkempt beard. He was wearing a tweed jacket and button-down shirt over jeans and hiking boots. He *wasn't* wearing a mask, which made no sense at all.

Luna moved to meet him, her hands coming up to grab for him fast enough that he couldn't even begin to jump back, or maybe he just didn't want to try. Even though he was a grown-up and she was just a kid, she had enough strength to hold him in place while her mouth opened wide and then wider still, a great cloud of vapor seeming to boil up in her throat as if waiting to be released. Feeling almost guilty, she breathed it out toward the man, enfolding him in a cloud of vapor thick enough to leave him coughing.

Luna stepped back, the aliens who controlled her obviously waiting for him to transform. He stood there, though, lifting the gun he held, and Luna felt a rush of fear. She might not feel pain, but she was pretty sure that if someone did enough damage to her, she would still be able to die. For a moment, she found herself hoping that the vapor she'd breathed out would take hold before he got a chance to fire. She didn't want to die. Then she felt guilty for even thinking that. She shouldn't wish this on anyone.

But the gun did not fire.

Instead, a cloud of blue-green vapor came out of the barrel, pouring into Luna's lungs with every breath. She started to reach out for him to snap his gun in half, and probably to do the same to him, but the strangest thing happened when her arms were less than halfway to him.

She stopped.

In a single moment, she froze in place, her heartbeat coming faster and faster. She felt her whole world spinning.

Luna fell to her knees involuntarily. She felt them scrape on the sidewalk, actually *felt* it, and the sensation coming back was like when blood rushed back in after an arm or a leg had gone to sleep. It hurt and she cried out.

She couldn't believe it.

She was back.

Back to her old self. No longer controlled.

She dug down into her memories, making sure they were still there; that they hadn't been lost completely. She pictured Kevin's face, and her parents as they had been on the first birthday she could remember. She breathed a sigh of relief, and not just for herself. It meant that the people who had been transformed weren't lost.

She wanted to shriek with joy. To reach out and hug this man and never let go.

She stared up at him in wonder.

He smiled down in a curious, academic way.

"My," he said, "you seem to be responding much quicker than the other subjects I've tried this on. Oh, forgive me, where are my manners? I'm Ignatius Gable. The vapor you just breathed in is the vaccine I created to counter the effects of the alien control. You should feel complete control returning to you shortly. Now, I'm sure you have a lot of questions about what's going on, but we're not exactly in a position to chat here. So unless we both want to get killed for good, I suggest you come with me."

She blinked back, startled, and followed his gaze to see countless controlled closing in.

"NOW!" he shouted.

The controlled started to descend on them in a swarm. Luna could only watch as they crowded in close, grabbing for them. He sprayed them with his gun, but for the others, it didn't seem to work.

Luna ran forward, plunging into the crowd and slipping through the spaces with every advantage she could get from being smaller than most of the people there. She ducked under arms and skidded between legs, taking Ignatius's arm and not letting go.

Luna spotted Cub, and Bear, and the rest of them, and she snatched the gun and whirled around.

"What are you doing?" he cried out in alarm.

She sprayed a cloud of it that started to slow the controlled around her, spraying Cub and Bear and all the rest of them.

"Come on," she said, as she kept her finger down on the trigger. "Change!"

Luna saw Cub blinking in the sunlight, stretching out his hands and staring at them.

She looked around until she saw Bobby in the shadows of a building and held out a hand to him.

And then she turned with the others and ran.

And didn't stop running.

CHAPTER FOUR

Kevin recoiled when Purest Xan came into the room that held him and Chloe. Hanging there alone and unattended was bad enough, but somehow he knew it wouldn't be as bad as anything the alien chose to do now.

"Fear is a weakness," Purest Xan said, the words coming out a moment later through its translator. "Just one of many we have conquered."

"What do you mean?" Kevin asked. He tried to hold back the fear he felt too, because he didn't want the alien to see it now.

Chloe looked scared enough for both of them, but she looked angry too. If the twisted gravity hadn't been there, holding them to the frames, Kevin suspected that she would have tried to attack the alien.

"Once, we were as weaker beings," Purest Xan said, making a gesture so that a section of wall shifted into a screen that showed things that were like the Purest and not like them, all at once. They weren't quite smooth-skinned, weren't quite as graceful or as perfect looking, and certainly didn't have the sense of cold implacability that the Purest had. They looked like the kind of things the Purest might have been a long, long time ago.

"We fought and we warred with one another. We turned our home world into a place that was almost unlivable with the weapons we used."

The image on the screen shifted, showing a world that started out green and beautiful, only for all of that plant life to wither and die, and explosions to ripple across the surface, with fire and tearing winds spreading out in ripples from what looked like the heart of cities.

"We had to find ways to adapt."

"By attacking other people's worlds," Kevin said. "By tricking us into letting you in so that you could take over people's minds."

"You're evil," Chloe added. "You're nothing but monsters."

Purest Xan looked at them without a hint of emotion. Kevin doubted that the creature was capable of them, and in some ways that was scarier than if Chloe had been right. These creatures weren't malicious, or filled with hate, or determined to wipe out everything they feared. They acted as coldly and calmly as a glacier rolling over a town, not caring about the lives within.

21

"Your worlds do not matter," Purest Xan said. "You are not of the Hive. You are not of the Purest."

"You really think you're the only things that matter in the universe?" Chloe demanded.

"We are the Purest," Xan replied, as if that answered everything. "We created the Hive to solve the wars of our world. In coming together, we learned to put ourselves beyond the weaknesses of emotion. We learned from the worlds nearest us how to transform the lesser to be all that we require them to be. We built the Hive ships to carry us and gather materials with which to regenerate our world for the Purest."

"So you just take and take, and give nothing back," Kevin said.

"All else is lesser," Purest Xan said. "All is ours."

"Until we stop you," Chloe said, struggling against the gravity that held her. If it felt anything like the shifted gravity that held Kevin in place, he knew that she had no chance of breaking free, but he guessed that telling her that wouldn't persuade her to stop. If anything, it would probably make things worse.

"You are weak. You cannot stop the Hive," Purest Xan said.

"Then why are we still here?" Kevin asked. "If you think we're so weak and useless, why didn't you have us killed the moment we arrived on your... ship?"

"We do not destroy what is useful," Purest Xan said. "We gather it. It is our purpose."

Useful. Kevin wasn't sure he liked the idea of being useful to something like this. From what he'd seen of the other creatures they had found useful, the aliens went around reshaping their flesh, transforming them. He'd already felt the pain involved just with the aliens going through his thoughts. The visions he'd seen of the aliens' world had been even worse.

"I don't want to be useful to you," Kevin said.

"You get no choice," Purest Xan said. "You should be grateful to us. The chosen of a world are typically destroyed, to stop them being... a danger to us. You survive because we permit you to survive."

"Why?" Kevin insisted.

Purest Xan didn't answer for a moment or two. Instead, the alien moved around the room, making adjustments to some of the machinery.

"They're going to look in our minds again, Kevin," Chloe said, sounding terrified by the prospect. "They're going to use those tentacle things again."

"Not on you," Purest Xan said, sounding almost contemptuous. "You will be intriguing enough to dissect and reshape. Your mind is quite interesting, but you are not worthy of more."

"You can't dissect Chloe!" Kevin yelled, fighting against the gravity that held him. It pressed him back into the frame easily, no matter how much he struggled to break free. The pressure held him flat, like a lead weight pressing down on his chest.

"We may do as we wish," Purest Xan said. "If that is the greatest use the female can be to the Hive, that is what will happen. We will be generous, though. You will get to choose what happens to her."

"Then I choose that she doesn't get dissected!" Kevin said.

"After we are done," Purest Xan said. "After you have joined our Hive."

"What?" Kevin said. He shook his head. "No way."

The alien moved to him, the tentacled devices ready in his hands.

"Your brain has capacities that the Hive requires," Purest Xan said. "Therefore you will join us."

The alien made it sound like an undeniable fact, as if it was simply the way the world was. It made the idea sound as obvious and natural as water being wet, or as the sun being hot. There was nothing natural about the tentacled *things* that Purest Xan held in its hands, though.

"So, what?" Kevin demanded, mostly because every moment he could delay this felt like a good idea. "You're going to make me into one of the Purest like you? Do I get to lose all of my hair and have freaky eyes?"

Maybe if Kevin could annoy the alien enough, he could distract it from what it was about to do. Of course, it might then decide to do a whole host of things that were even worse, but right then, Kevin couldn't *think* of anything worse than being changed into one of them.

"You are not of the Purest," Purest Xan said. "But you can be made of the Hive. You will become our emissary, one of *our* chosen. You should welcome the honor."

"You think it's some kind of honor for Kevin to have his brain invaded?" Chloe demanded.

"It will not be an invasion," Purest Xan said. "Kevin will welcome us. He will *agree* to become one of us."

"Why do I have to agree?" Kevin demanded. "Why don't you just do it if you're going to, instead of playing games?"

The alien looked almost offended by that, although Kevin doubted that it could feel that emotion either. He doubted that it could feel anything.

"We do not play games," it said. "Your species' brains are delicate, though, and we require yours intact for the tasks that the Hive has for you. If you fight too much during the process, there is the potential that you could be... damaged."

"I'll fight you," Kevin promised. "I'll die rather than do anything to help you."

The alien stood there staring at him, apparently not comprehending what he had just said. It frowned at Kevin slightly, tilting its head to one side as though listening to something only it could hear. Kevin got the feeling that it was trying to make sense of him, and trying to work out what to do while it did so.

"Your statement is foolish," Purest Xan said. "Yielding is to your advantage. You get to continue to exist."

"I'm dying anyway," Kevin said, thinking about the moment when the doctor had diagnosed him with his illness, had told him just how little time he had left to live. "Do you think I care about threats?"

The alien stared at him for another moment or two, and again, Kevin had the sense of it getting advice from the others of its kind.

"We can save you," it said, dropping the words there like lead weights.

The shock of that ran through Kevin like ice water. The best scientists Earth had to offer had tried and failed to help him. Now here the aliens were, offering to make him well as if it were nothing.

"You're lying," he said. He had to believe that they were lying. "You already lied about so much, do you think I'm going to believe this?"

He thought about all the ways they'd lied to get him to help with their invasion of the Earth. They'd told him that they were refugees seeking the safety of another planet. They'd told him that they were the ones fleeing destruction, rather than causing it.

"You have seen what we can do," Purest Xan said. "We can manipulate flesh in ways your human mind cannot imagine. The Purest of the Hive are preserved almost indefinitely. We have every reason to want you alive. We could heal you, if you were of the Hive."

What could Kevin say to that kind of temptation? It was everything he had wanted from the moment the doctor had told him what was happening. When he'd been at the NASA institute, he'd secretly hoped that one of the scientists there might find some way to help him, to make all the shaking and the pain stop. He'd thought that he would give almost anything to be well again. It took almost everything Kevin had to shake his head.

"If I have to die to stop you getting what you want, then that's what I'll do," Kevin said. He meant it. He wanted to live, he'd hoped for a cure, but by now, he'd had plenty of time to accept what was going to happen to him. If dying could help to stop the aliens... well, he didn't *want* to, but he would.

"And what about the other things the Hive can offer?" Purest Xan said. "We are told that your species values parents and friends. As one of us, you could decide what was done with those we controlled."

Kevin swallowed, thinking of his mother, thinking of Luna. There were so many people he knew back on Earth, so far away that it was no longer visible on the screen. If he could help them... no, if the aliens wanted something from him, that wouldn't help them at all.

"Then there is the question of your friend here," Purest Xan said. "As this one has said, as one of the Hive, you could determine what happens to her. If you do not do this, the female will be experimented on while you watch."

Kevin froze, looking from the alien to Chloe and back.

"No, Kevin. Don't do it," Chloe said. Kevin could hear the desperation there. "Let them kill me. Do whatever it takes!"

Kevin could hear the sincerity in her voice, but... he couldn't do it. He couldn't stand there and watch while Chloe died. He knew that they would do it. There was something about the cold, emotionless way Xan made its threat that made it something else. Not a threat exactly, more a simple statement of what would happen.

"We will change you anyway," Purest Xan said. "It is simply a question of how much you fight, and how much it hurts. Make your decision, Kevin McKenzie."

"Fight them, Kevin," Chloe said. "Don't give in!"

Kevin looked at her, trying not to think of all the things the aliens might do to her. It was impossible, though, to do anything but picture what might happen once they started to experiment on her. Could he really stand by and watch if they started to take her apart to see how she worked, or started to transform her into something that wasn't human? Could he do that, when all it would mean was that they would transform him by force?

He couldn't, and he knew it.

"Okay," he said, hating every moment while he did it. "Do it."

"We were always going to," Purest Xan assured him. "This will hurt more, the more you struggle."

"Kevin," Chloe said. "Please fight it. You have to stay yourself. You have to stay strong."

That, Kevin guessed, was the only hope here. They couldn't break free. They couldn't fight back physically. The only chance was to join with the Hive, and somehow hope to retain enough of himself...

He didn't even finish that thought before Purest Xan applied the tentacles to his skull, and the Hive lanced invisibly into his brain.

Kevin cried out with the pain, swift and sudden, like an icicle being stabbed into the depths of his mind. He'd thought that he was used to pain; with his illness, he'd thought he'd known what pain was, but now he realized that it was nothing compared to what was happening now. He could feel the tentacles questing through his thoughts and his memories, the unpleasant sensation far too familiar from when the aliens had first probed his mind.

This was different, though, because the aliens weren't just looking this time.

Kevin could feel the Hive inside his thoughts, mind upon mind, interlinked and powerful. It was hot and cold and painful all at the same time. It felt like ground glass being worked through his thoughts. He could feel the wash of the controlled on the far fringes, not even a true part of the whole. He could feel the sharp-edged minds of things bred for war, and the softer, slower thoughts of beasts of burden. Then there were the Purest and their servants, shining strands against the web of the rest.

Come to us, they urged, the voices deep and seductive. *Become us.*

Kevin tried to pull away, and the effort hurt more than he could have imagined. He heard himself scream, but the sound seemed to come to him from far away. It was like claws holding him in place, hooked into his brain, too powerful to ignore.

Even so, Kevin fought. He could feel the Hive moving through him, taking over parts of his mind the way an invading army might take over fields and towns. Kevin started to hide parts of himself, remembering the way he'd tried to hide how scared he was for his mother's benefit, trying to hide away whatever he could while the aliens continued to push forward within his mind. If he could do it enough, he might be able to hold himself separate from the Hive. He might still be himself.

He felt the moment when they linked him to the Hive, going from seeing all the separate strands to being one of them. He could hear the messages and the thoughts of the others there, the commands of the Purest and the obedience of the rest.

A mind that picks things apart, one of the Purest thought in his direction.

A mind that is everything we need, another agreed.

Kevin could feel Purest Xan's presence beside him. *Wake, Kevin, join your new life.*

Kevin's eyes snapped open, and he couldn't remember closing them. The world around him looked strange, cloaked in a sheen of new colors, details he would never have noticed before coming to his eyes. It was as if he could focus on every mote of dust and fraction of color change.

He looked around at the machines, and the Hive within him told him what each was for. Had he succeeded in holding back some part of himself? Kevin didn't know. He still *felt* like himself, although everything else about the world seemed strange. It seemed both more alive and more connected than he could have ever imagined.

Purest Xan moved to him, working the controls on the frame. The alien operated them, and Kevin felt the gravity that was holding him in place shift back toward the floor.

"Welcome to the Hive, Emissary Kevin," Purest Xan said.

CHAPTER FIVE

Luna and the bikers ran from the controlled as they closed in, lunging for their bikes, trying to make it to them before the greater speed of those the aliens controlled brought them too close. Luna ran toward the spot where her own bike had stopped, lying on its side now with the sidecar up in the air, obviously overturned in whatever chaos had followed the moment when they'd grabbed her.

She struggled to right it, shoving her entire body against it, the weight of it making it feel as though she was pushing against a solid wall. Luna felt it shift slightly as she kept pushing, and then it toppled, raising a small cloud of dust as it hit the ground beside the road.

"Get in, Bobby," she called to the dog, who was still busy growling at the advancing horde of controlled as if he might be able to fend them off. "Hurry!"

She pointed to the sidecar, and the dog got the message, hopping into it and sitting there, looking around with his teeth bared. Looking back, Luna could see why: the controlled were getting closer, running in that way that put them far closer than they should have been every time she blinked. Luna went to start the bike, determined to put as much distance between her and the controlled as possible...

It wouldn't start.

"Not now," Luna said through gritted teeth as the engine coughed and spluttered. "Come *on!*"

She jumped her entire weight on the kick-starter once, then again. She could see the controlled getting closer now, so that they were twenty yards away, then ten. Luna could feel the fear building in her. She really didn't want to know what the controlled would do to someone who wasn't one of them anymore.

She jumped on the starter once more, throwing her whole weight down onto it, and the bike roared into life. Luna didn't hesitate, accelerating as hard as she dared away from the onrushing crowd of controlled people. She felt the heaviness as an unfeeling hand clamped onto her bike, a woman with unseeing white pupils holding on tight enough that the bike dragged her along, making her skid along the ground when even her enhanced speed wasn't enough to keep up.

Luna found herself trying to remember if she'd seen this woman while they'd all been forced to work. She found herself thinking about the person who might still be trapped somewhere behind those eyes, the person who might be fighting to stop herself even as she reached for Luna. Luna knew exactly how bad it was to be one of the controlled now, and she knew that there was nothing the person in there could do to stop themselves.

On the other hand, she knew that they didn't feel pain.

"Sorry," Luna said, kicking out at the woman from her perch on the bike until the controlled woman tumbled back onto the road, letting Luna's bike shoot forward fast enough that she had to cling to it tightly so she didn't fall off.

Around her, Luna saw the members of the Dustsides Motorcycle Club grabbing their bikes and pulling away in formation, the bikes forming a broad V shape as if they might be able to smash through anything that got in their way. She saw Ignatius jump onto the back of Bear's bike, still clutching his precious vapor gun.

There were more controlled coming out of side streets now, lunging for the bikes from every direction. The only hope seemed to be to keep going as fast as possible, hoping that sheer speed would carry them past the mass of the controlled before they could close in on them like water pouring into a basin. Luna was fine with going faster. Being scared of the sheer speed was definitely better than thinking about the prospect of being torn apart by the controlled.

"Don't stop!" Luna called out to the others, as loud as she could so that it would carry over the noise of the bikes. "We need to get away."

They kept riding, as fast as possible. With the controlled approaching from the back and the sides, their bikes popped out of the mass of them like a cork from a bottle. In an instant, they were in clear space, hurrying through Sedona, trying to get as far from the onrushing horde of controlled as they could. They were moving faster than the controlled could follow now, heading for the outskirts of the town.

"I think we're clear," Cub called back with a grin that said how happy he was to be free of the aliens' control.

Luna smiled back at him, because she was just as happy to have made it. She was happy that *he* had been saved too. She wouldn't have liked the idea of Cub still being back there while she and the others got away. She rode up closer to him, ready to call across to him, although she wasn't quite sure what she was going to call. Maybe that she was glad he was there, maybe more than that.

29

Whatever she was going to say, the words fell silent in her throat as the shine of something up in the sky caught her eye, growing larger by the moment.

"A ship!" Luna called out as she looked at it square on.

The ship was one of the smaller ones, but this one looked sleeker than the others somehow, and more dangerous. If the others were worker bees built for carrying things up to the bigger ships, this one seemed more like a hornet, sharp-edged and deadly, designed to kill anything that got in its way.

"It's coming this way!" Luna shouted.

It came in rapidly, and Luna found herself wondering where it had come from. The big ship above Sedona was gone. Even the world ship that had been there was gone, vanished from the sky as rapidly as it had come. This one must have come from one of the other ships, still hovering over other towns and cities to take what they could. From the speed it was coming in, it must have shot toward them as fast as its engines would carry it.

"They've sent a ship from another city for *us*?" Cub called out.

It didn't make any sense that a ship could be there for them that fast, or that they could possibly mean that much to the aliens. Yet she couldn't think of another reason why a ship like that would be coming toward them so fast, or so low, just a few hundred feet off the ground. Them coming back from being controlled seemed to have upset the aliens more than anything else they could have done.

"They must have sensed people breaking out of their control," Luna called.

"I have found that the controlled hurry in quickly towards my efforts," Ignatius explained from the back of Bear's bike. "I think they're trying to stop my attempts to help people."

Luna thought about the aliens who had controlled her. How would they react to people breaking free of them? How would they respond to any loss of control when all they seemed to want was to *take* more and more?

Luna thought she saw something starting to glow at the front of the ship, a fiery orange that made it look as though someone had set light to a point on the vessel's nose. She tried to decide if it might be a trick of the light, and then a far more horrible thought occurred to her.

"Everybody scatter!" she yelled, pulling her bike to one side so fast that it took everything she had to keep it upright.

The road ahead of their small convoy erupted in a blaze of energy that tore through the asphalt, sending dirt and stone flying in every direction. Luna saw one of the bikes skid and topple, the rider tumbling over the ground as the road disappeared from under them.

Luna went off road, ignoring the jolts and the judders that came from the uneven ground as rocks and potholes threatened to unseat her. Around her, she could see the other bikes following, heading into the rougher terrain, staying away from the straight line of the road as the alien ship shrieked overhead. Another gout of dirt and rocks flew up as it fired again, and then it was past them, banking sharply as it started to turn back toward them.

They were an easy target in the open. Luna could see the alien ship getting further away from them, lining up another run at them. If it fired at them from a distance, it would have plenty of time to aim and hit them all. They needed to find cover, and they needed to do it *now*.

Luna looked around and then pointed toward some of the red rock valleys close to Sedona.

"There!" she yelled. "It's our only hope."

She pushed her engine, the bike speeding forward with the others following in her wake. Dirt exploded around them as the ship made another pass, and for a moment or two Luna couldn't see anything ahead. When the cloud of dust cleared enough for her to see again, she had to veer left sharply to avoid the remains of a tree, torn apart by the latest blast. Luna just hoped that she was leading the others in the right direction.

They headed into the valley, plunging past its mouth and speeding down it. Energy bolts slammed into the walls, sending dust up into the air and sending rocks tumbling so that Luna had to swerve and dodge to avoid them. They rumbled and bounced as they fell, one shooting past her head, close enough that she had to duck down to avoid it.

"It's coming in lower!" Cub called out from somewhere close to Luna. Luna knew that she ought to keep her eyes on the way ahead through the valley, but she couldn't stop herself from risking a glance back.

The alien ship was flying barely above ground level now, moving into the valley on their tail as it tried to line up its next shots.

"Faster," Luna called out.

"We can't lose it," Cub called back.

"We don't need to lose it," Luna shouted. "We just need to find out how fast it can turn."

She saw Cub grin as he understood, and their group of bikers hurried forward, pushing into the valley.

"Hold on, Bobby," Luna said.

Luna clung to her bike, taking the twists and turns as fast as she dared, then faster still. The red rocks of the cliffs towered above her in misshapen stacks, the rocks that tumbled as energy blasts hit them a reminder of just how easily all of this could go wrong. One turn taken too fast, one twitch of the handlebars in the wrong direction, and she and Bobby would hammer into the walls of the valley, far too fast to survive.

Luna gripped her handlebars tight, hunched down over them, and rode faster.

She dared a glance back. The alien ship was still there, taking the twists and turns with them, firing at random when it couldn't line up the perfect shot. It swung from one side to the other as it sped along the valley, and then, without warning, Luna saw one edge of it clip a wall.

"Watch out!" she yelled, as it bounced from one wall to the next, struggling to correct its flight as it ricocheted like a pool ball, sparks flying as it hit one wall, then another, angling down toward the valley's rocky floor.

The noise as it struck the earth seemed to fill the world, dust flying up as it plowed in nose first until everything behind it was obscured. Luna and the others had to keep riding flat out just to stay ahead of it. They were running out of room, though, because the valley was coming to a halt, sealed in by a wall of rock that was punctured only by the opening of a storm drain. Luna rode toward that far end, hoping the ship would stop before it crushed them all against the wall. She pulled up next to the wall, wincing as the ship got closer.

Gradually, though, it slowed, squealing and scraping its way along like a plate dropped from a table until finally, rattling, it ground to a halt.

Luna pulled up in front of it, the others spreading out in a half circle around it, engines still running. She heard a hiss of escaping air as a hatch near the top opened, and she stood in shock as a figure staggered out.

This wasn't one of the controlled. There was nothing human about the spindly, insect-like figure who clambered down from the hatch, spiny plates looking like armor, but broken armor, with rents that leaked clear fluid onto the ground as it advanced.

"Is that them?" she heard Ignatius wonder aloud. "Is that what the aliens look like?"

"Does it matter what they look like when we know what they want?" Luna asked.

"But we can study it," Ignatius said. "We need to try to capture it."

It kept approaching, reaching for them as if even now it would find a way to kill them.

"Get it!" Bear yelled, and the Dustsides bikers fell on it with fists and pipes and knives, striking again and again with anything they had. Luna heard the armored plates crack with a sickening sound that reminded Luna far too much of someone stepping on a beetle.

"No," Ignatius said, "there's so much we can *learn*."

Right then, however, Luna felt as though they'd learned the most important lessons: they'd learned what one of their enemies looked like, and they'd learned that they could die.

Then a light flickered on the front of the ship, twisting in the air, taking the shape of a tall, hairless figure that looked nothing like the creature they had just killed. It spoke, and some technology in the hologram translated the words, the same way it had with the boxes at the slave camp.

"You have killed one of our servants," the being said. "But it is not of the Purest. It does not matter. You do not matter. You are an obstruction to be removed, and you will be, unless you submit now."

"We know what that feels like," Luna shouted back at it. "And we broke free. We're going to break *everyone* free!"

"You will not obstruct the Hive. You will die."

It flickered out of sight, and in the sky beyond where it had been, Luna thought she could see the specks of more of the ships closing in. It seemed that the aliens weren't holding back when it came to killing them.

"We need to get out of here," Luna said.

"There's no easy way past the ship," Cub said, "and if we ride out onto open ground, they'll pick us off easily."

"Then we need to go into the storm drain," Luna said.

Bear looked over at it, then at her and Cub. "I don't like leaving the bikes."

"I think it's that or die, Dad," Cub said.

"What do you think?" he asked Luna.

Luna was surprised by that. Bear was the bikers' leader. Then again, she'd been the one to lead them into the valley. Maybe they assumed that she knew what she was doing.

"I don't think we have a choice," she said.

Bear nodded. "I guess not."

"Ignatius," Luna said. "What I said before to that *thing*... we *can* save everyone, can't we?"

"I think that's something we need to talk about once we're safe," Ignatius said. "I'll explain everything, but not here, okay?"

"Okay," Luna said, with a look back at where the alien ships were closing in. The only question now was whether they would ever be safe again.

She ran forward into the storm drain. Behind her, she could hear the first explosions as the aliens opened fire.

CHAPTER SIX

Kevin could feel the full beauty and weight of the Hive buzzing in his brain. No, that wasn't right. It wasn't in him; he was in *it*. He was one part of the whole, a mote of light in a whole interconnected galaxy. Trying to keep track of it all was dizzying, seemingly impossible.

"It will get easier," Purest Xan promised him, although there was no kindness or sympathy in that. It was simply an observation of fact.

"Has the Hive always been so... big?" Kevin asked, barely able to comprehend the scale of everything that he could feel.

"You are seeing the connections of one world ship," Purest Xan said. "Look beyond, Kevin."

Kevin tried to look deeper, and now he saw a shining strand leading out from the Hive that he was connected to, linking to a bigger, more complex web of connections in turn: a Hive of Hives, stretching so far out that just trying to comprehend the scale of it made Kevin's eyes water with the effort.

"The Hive is what matters," Purest Xan said. "We serve the Hive, and the Hive exists to preserve those of us who are still pure, still what we once were. Do you understand?"

In that moment, Kevin did. He understood it in a way that had nothing to do with words, or logic, or anything else that he would have understood before. He felt the need of the Hive to survive, built from the need of the Purest to preserve themselves and their world, whatever the cost to the rest of the universe. He understood the need to be a part of it, and to contribute to it all. He could see the pockets of thoughts there, and memories, the clusters of minds that worked on different projects, whole banks of them given over to calculations or contemplation. A part of him wanted to delve into those pockets, losing himself completely in their depths.

"Come with me," Purest Xan said, drawing Kevin away from the complex web of the Hive's connections. They were still there, he was still connected to them so completely that it was impossible to think that the world had ever been any other way, but now he was able to focus on his own body enough to move and follow, stepping in the alien's wake.

Purest Xan led the way from the room, up through the spire, almost all the way to the top. From up there, it was possible to see out toward the other spires of the world ship, standing golden and pure among the grim grayness of the rest of it.

"Stand here," the alien said, gesturing to a round disc on the floor that Xan stood on, golden and solid looking. Kevin stood there without hesitation.

It lifted into the air, silently and smoothly, still feeling as solid underfoot as the ground had.

"How does this work?" Kevin asked.

"It is a simple matter of gravity propulsion," Purest Xan replied. "If you require more knowledge of it, the details will sit within the Hive."

That idea filled Kevin with wonder. He hadn't considered that the connections between minds he'd seen would be more than that.

"So it's like an internet of brains?" he asked.

Purest Xan was still for a moment, and Kevin felt the barest brush of a mind against his as the alien tried to understand the word.

"Yes, that is almost correct," the alien replied. "The knowledge that the Hive holds can be accessed by any. It is a part of us, though, not some external store."

Kevin tried to picture the idea of being able to access clusters of other minds at will, and then realized that he didn't have to imagine it. The Hive was there, and all he had to do was reach out to access it.

"Later," Purest Xan said. "For now, there is more to see."

"Did your people invent this disc?" Kevin asked, as the platform continued to float over the city.

"It was another thing learned from a conquered world," Purest Xan said. "Their people were unworthy to survive except as materials, but knowledge such as this must be collected and put to the use of the Hive."

Kevin felt as though he ought to have been horrified by the alien's words, but he didn't feel any of that horror. He didn't feel much of anything beyond the beauty of the Hive.

"How does the Hive work?" Kevin asked.

"You could see it, if you looked for the knowledge," Purest Xan pointed out, "but it is right that we should explain." The alien gestured to the golden spires that stuck out from the interior of the world ship. "These are the homes of the Purest. We guide the rest of the Hive, and give it purpose. You have already seen the interior of one spire. The others will be similar."

Their golden disc floated down now, into one of the complexes of the seemingly endless city that surrounded the spire. There were glass-walled greenhouses there, more like factories than farms,

36

filled with vats and rows of growing things, stacked one atop another. Spiderlike creatures crawled through them, and Kevin could see them tending to the crops within. Reaching out toward them through the Hive, Kevin could see that they were little more than mindless drones, there to receive orders.

"These are the nutrition factories," Purest Xan said. "The creatures within are changed versions of the ones who first created them. Their world was a thing of narrow caves, and needed factories like this to produce enough to feed them. Now they feed the Hive."

Xan made it sound like a blessing, as though their world had only been waiting for the opportunity to serve the Hive in any way that it could be used. He even understood it, sensing the importance of the Hive, and the need for every resource to be used for its benefit. If a world could supply nutrient farms and workers, then wasn't it right that it should?

"The farms are only the beginning," Purest Xan promised, and Kevin could hardly wait to see what might be next in that case.

Their platform continued down through the contours of the world ship, into a space where it seemed that things were in the process of being constructed. Kevin could see hordes of creatures scuttling over spaceships like ants over a nest, fastening pieces into place in shapes that were almost too complex to make sense of.

He could see others working on what looked like energy weapons, calibrating them and testing them in flashes that lit up the interior of the ship further.

"The creatures who possessed this did not even see the possibility of using this technology as a weapon," Purest Xan said. "They were peaceful things."

The alien made "peaceful" sound like a curse.

Kevin could see workshops down there, and spaces where the creatures of the Hive worked on technologies he couldn't begin to understand... and that he then did, reaching into the Hive for the knowledge. Waves of knowledge flooded into him about materials stronger than anything on Earth, about dust mote–sized robots, and weapons designed to overcome beings he hadn't even known existed until that moment. It was hard to hold onto all of that knowledge, or even to truly understand it, but it was there.

Kevin could see all the individual pieces that went together to make the world ship function, and it seemed incredible that it could fit together so well.

"We integrated each piece into the Hive as we found it," Purest Xan said.

Kevin suspected that "found" meant the same thing as "took" here. The Hive stole whatever it needed, whatever it saw, from the worlds that it encountered.

"Have you found new technologies on Earth?" Kevin asked.

The alien made a dismissive noise, as if the very idea that there was anything to learn from Earth was ludicrous.

"Then why come to Earth?" Kevin asked. "What did you gain?"

"That is a fair question," Purest Xan said. The golden disc that the two of them stood upon changed direction, heading toward an area of the world ship that seemed to burn with the heat of forges and smelts, where warehouses and yawning pits of goods stood.

Below, Kevin could see worker aliens built with muscles and claws that could tear apart rocks and rip through steel. There were small, nimble things that could pick through piles of collected detritus, seeking out the smallest quantities of rare metals and unusual elements. They were loading floating carts by the spaces that they worked, for iron and calcium, wood and glass. There were barrels for water and other liquids, from the juice of fruits to the acids produced in its factories, while canisters stood there to hold gasses siphoned off from any world they encountered: oxygen and helium, radon and stranger things.

Kevin watched the aliens below picking apart things that had presumably been taken from his world, and he felt… nothing, had no response to the strange rapaciousness of it all.

"Why don't I feel anything?" he asked. "You're tearing apart things taken from my world, and I don't feel anything."

"Your former world," Purest Xan corrected him. "You are of the Hive now, Kevin. We have made you a part of us, and you no longer have to fear such human weaknesses."

It hadn't felt like a weakness to Kevin before to feel things, but now he could see how obvious it was that it *was* a weakness. Had he still been held back by human feelings, he wouldn't have been able to stand by and watch the resources of his world being plundered like this. He would have felt obliged to intervene, and then, no doubt, the creatures of the Hive would have killed him.

"You have made me strong," Kevin said.

"Strong enough to fulfill your purpose for the Hive. Strong enough to serve it," Purest Xan said.

"Do you do that for all the creatures you take?" Kevin asked.

Purest Xan made that amused, dismissive sound again. "Most are too weak to be anything but meat to shape. Come, I will show you."

They flew toward a new space now, and in this space, Kevin could hear the screams of a hundred or more different kinds of creatures, translated only because his mind seemed to grab onto them automatically and understand.

"Remarkable," Purest Xan said with a look across at him. "Your brain is exactly what the Hive needs, Kevin McKenzie."

The alien seemed unbothered that below them, creature after creature was crying out in agony. It didn't seem to matter that there were some being taken apart while still alive and others being put back together into new shapes, that there were benches there where aliens and animals and even some people lay while members of the Purest worked on them.

Then again, Kevin himself wasn't bothered the way he probably should have been. He had a feeling that the sight of a man having his skin replaced in patches with what looked like grafts from other species ought to make him feel sick and angry and filled with hate toward creatures that could do something like that, but instead, he just looked at it, noting the results.

"Our flesh factories are complex places," Purest Xan said. "The manipulations there are the oldest skills that we mastered, some even before we became the Hive. In each place we go, we seek the strongest DNA, the most useful traits. It is why we seek out planets that teem with life, rather than mining barren rocks."

They went closer to the flesh factory, and Kevin could see clear cages with animals taken from every corner of the Earth, already starting to be twisted by the things the Hive's aliens were doing to them. A dolphin swam, a pair of horns curling from its head. A chimp seemed to have metal implants running through its skin.

"What's the point of all this?" Kevin asked. "What are you trying to achieve with it?"

It looked like mindless cruelty, doing evil things for their own sake, or at least things that Kevin had always been taught were evil. Now, the distinction no longer seemed quite so clear cut.

"Perfection," Purest Xan said. "We seek perfection by exploring what every species has to give. We learn and we improve, so that we will be able to survive anything that afflicts us. We will not be driven to the brink of extinction again. We augment ourselves, crafting servants and living devices. Soon, you will be given the tools you need to serve the Hive."

"You're going to transform me?" Kevin said. He didn't feel fear. There was no part of him left now that could.

"As little as necessary," Purest Xan said. "We do not wish to risk harming that which makes you useful. Now, we should return. The Hive made a promise to you."

"A promise?" Kevin asked, as the golden disc turned back toward the spire it had come from.

"Regarding the female human."

Chloe. Kevin had somehow completely forgotten about Chloe. His thoughts should have been filled with concern for her, worries about what might be happening to her while he was gone. Instead, he'd walked from the room like she didn't even exist, and hadn't even thought about her since. What was he doing? What was wrong with him?

"There is nothing wrong with you, Kevin," Purest Xan said, answering his thoughts in a way that reminded Kevin just how deep the connection to the Hive ran. "You have merely seen that some things are more important. Come."

They landed on the spire, and Purest Xan led the way from the disc down into it.

"I feel…" Kevin began. "I feel as though I should hate you. As though I should want to fight you."

"And *do* you feel those things?" Purest Xan asked, although surely the alien must have known the answer to that right then.

"No," Kevin admitted.

"Then all is well," Purest Xan said simply. The alien led the way back down to the room where they had held Kevin.

Chloe was still there, still pinned in place to the frame that held her by the weight of gravity.

"Kevin, you came back," she said as he entered the room, sounding relieved that he was there. "I've had to stay here waiting for them to come and torture me."

"Not torture you," Kevin said. "I've seen what they do here, Chloe. They would experiment on you to understand you, then probably take you apart and rebuild you."

Chloe stared at him. "Why are you saying all that like it doesn't matter?" she demanded. "What's wrong with you, Kevin?"

Kevin shook his head. Of course Chloe couldn't understand. She wasn't a part of the Hive.

"There's nothing wrong with me."

"Tell them to let me go then, and we'll get out of here."

Once, not that long ago, Kevin would have done exactly that. He would have done anything for Chloe, and would have put himself in danger to protect her without a second thought. Now, it was hard for him to see why. Chloe wasn't a part of the Hive, and it wasn't as though he felt anything when he looked at her. Feeling things was for the weak.

"It is your decision," Purest Xan said. "Do you wish us to release her?"

"Does the Hive have a purpose for her?" Kevin asked.

Chloe frowned at him. "Kevin, what are you doing? Why are you talking to that thing like it's your friend? *We're* friends, remember?"

Kevin could remember, but he couldn't understand it. Why would he be friends with someone who wasn't a part of the Hive?

"It may be intriguing to experiment on her," Purest Xan said. "There are facets to her thoughts that some of the Purest have expressed an interest in, or perhaps she can be hybridized with some other creature, or vivisected."

"Kevin," Chloe called out. "You can't let them do this. I know you're in there somewhere. Fight this, Kevin! You have to fight back. You can't let them do this!"

"It is what is best for the Hive," Kevin told her. He returned his attention to Purest Xan. "Do what you want with her. I don't care about her."

CHAPTER SEVEN

Luna and the others hurried forward into the storm drains, trying to get away from the spot where they had left the bikes, and the sound of energy blasts striking the ground. Luna kept near Ignatius, because she wasn't going to let someone who could help to end this out of her sight, and Cub, because... well, *because*. Bobby walked along in her wake, close enough that Luna could feel the brush of his fur.

Luna and Bobby led the way because Luna was good at finding her way through spaces she hadn't explored yet. Bear followed, and the storm drains were big enough that even the bikers' leader didn't have to hunch over to make it through. The rest of the bikers brought up the rear, some looking back, some keeping whatever weapons they had out in readiness for a fight. Luna wasn't sure what those weapons would do against alien energy bursts, but she guessed that they needed all the help they could get. A few had flashlights, and it was quickly the only light they had in the concrete tunnels.

"This way," Luna said, hearing her voice echo through the storm drains. The network of them seemed to be as complicated as any cave system, and there were spots where she suspected it linked to the natural caves around Sedona, concrete giving way to the red rock that she recognized from the valley.

"Why that way?" Cub asked.

"Can't you feel the breeze?" Luna said, holding up a hand so she could feel the air currents on either side of it. "I think there's an exit somewhere up here."

"Okay, that makes sense," Cub said. "What do you think, Dad?"

Bear shrugged quietly, and that seemed to be enough of a signal for them all to keep going. They moved along in near silence, without even the drip of water since there didn't seem to have been any rain recently. Then Luna heard another sound, echoing far too loudly in the concrete environment of the storm drain: Bobby growling at something behind them, followed by a shriek that seemed to have come from something that had never been human.

"Something's coming," Luna said. "Run!"

She led the way through the tunnels, taking turnings almost at random now. Almost, because wherever she saw red rock, she

42

headed that way, guessing that the natural caves would be more confusing for whatever was following. Luna found a space where the caves curled around, creating a ledge that overlooked the main passage, and she pressed herself flat against the wall up there, looking down from between a couple of outcrops of rock.

"Here," she whispered, "hide, and kill the flashlights. Bobby, sit, be quiet."

The bikers did as she said, crouching down in whatever cover they could find and turning off their flashlights so that the cave was almost entirely dark. Luna heard the sound of things approaching with a steady clicking of something on the stone that didn't sound like shoes. A faint, greenish glow started to suffuse the space they were in, and Luna caught glimpses of things moving below. She couldn't see them well, but she could make out enough to suggest awful, spike-limbed things, moving jerkily and fast, scuttling through the space, navigating by a glow that seemed to come from within them.

Luna held her breath, holding onto Bobby's collar and not daring to make a sound as the creatures moved below her and the bikers. She froze in position, not wanting the least movement to betray her as the creatures lingered in the cavern space, as if sensing that something was wrong.

A small animal, a rat or a hare, burst from cover nearby. Instantly, the creatures spun toward it. One lanced down a long, deadly limb, and the animal died, pierced through. The alien things moved on then, but it was another ten minutes before Luna finally dared to breathe a sigh of relief.

"I think they're gone," she said. Bobby leapt down onto the floor of the cave.

"*Another* alien type," Ignatius said, sounding almost excited by the prospect. "How many are there, do you think?"

"Too many," Cub said. "Right, Dad?"

Bear grunted an affirmation.

They slipped back down into the complex of caves and storm drains, trying to work out the best way to go from there. Luna had always been pretty good at not losing her way when she went into some new space to explore, but even for her the caves were a challenge, *especially* when there might still be aliens around. She moved cautiously, picking her route with care and listening hard for any sign of the aliens that had been hunting for them.

Luna couldn't hear anything; it seemed as though they had swept through the tunnels as swiftly as the rainwater that they were designed to clear. Even so, she didn't relax until they were almost all the way through, finding a junction near one of the exits with a view out onto the city limits beyond.

"It's getting dark," Luna said, feeling surprised to find an evening sky out beyond the tunnels. "I didn't think we were in there that long."

"Without seeing the sun, it can be easy to lose track of time," Ignatius said.

"And we don't know how long we were changed into those things," Cub said. "I felt as though I was just gone, you know? I mean, I tried to fight it for a while, but then it was like there was nothing left of me. I was just asleep."

"I guess," Luna said. It hadn't been like that for her. She'd still been there, trapped beneath the surface, looking out, but she'd felt the pieces of herself fading away. Maybe what Cub described was what happened when that process finished.

"Maybe we should camp here until morning," Cub suggested. "We don't want to risk running into any of those things in the dark. What do you think, Dad?"

They all looked over to Bear. The bikers there followed him, after all. He shrugged. Luna could see beads of sweat on his forehead.

"Yeah, I guess," he said.

It seemed to be all he was willing to say right then, which meant that Luna and Cub had to decide what to do next. At least the bikers were willing to listen to what Cub said.

"It will be dry here if it doesn't rain too much." Luna said. "We'll have some shelter."

"We have some food with us," Cub said. "I think we can risk a fire. We'll need it once night falls and the temperature drops." He turned to some of the bikers clustered there. "Go get firewood, and see what else you can find that will be useful. Don't stray too far."

They set off, obeying his orders as quickly as they might have obeyed his father's. Luna had to admit that she was a little impressed.

She stepped outside, taking Bobby with her since she guessed that the dog wouldn't like being cooped up inside for too long. She looked up at the sky and breathed in the cool evening air. Looking up like that, she might have been able to believe that there was nothing wrong with the world: the alien world ship was gone, and there was no sign of any of the smaller ships flitting about, looking for resources to take. That absence hurt, though, enough that Luna could feel tears beading at the corners of her eyes, falling silently only because she didn't want the others to notice.

44

At least one person *did* notice, though.

"Hey, what is it?" Cub asked, reaching out to brush a tear away from her cheek with the pad of one thumb.

"You know that I hate that you've seen me cry, right?" Luna said. "I'm tougher than that. I don't break down all the time."

"Sometimes there are things worth crying about," Cub said. "Like being made into an alien puppet, or the world changing completely, or your friends being taken up into an alien spaceship."

"An alien spaceship that isn't even *there* anymore," Luna corrected him. If the world ship had still been up there, she might have been able to imagine Kevin and even Chloe working hard to get back. Instead, it was gone, and them with it. It felt as final as anything that had happened to her parents, or her other friends. It felt as though all the hope for them had vanished the moment the ship had.

"It will be okay," Cub told her, putting his arms around her.

Luna forced a smile. "You're really not doing your tough biker image any good, going around hugging people."

She was glad he did, though, because right then it felt as though the rest of the world was falling apart. Luna had been so sure that this would end with her and Kevin and Chloe all standing together, and now it felt almost the same as if they had died. For all she knew, they might have, or worse, up on the world ship. Not knowing didn't make it any better.

"We should go back inside," Cub said at last. "If you feel like you're ready? If you're okay?"

Luna wasn't sure she would ever truly be okay after this. Too much had happened in too short a space of time, and she seemed to be caught up in things far too deeply, given that she was only thirteen. She was ready to go back though. She wasn't going to give up now.

"I'm ready to hear what Ignatius has to say," Luna said. "If there's a way to help people, I want to know about it."

"Me too," Cub said.

They went back into the storm drain, where the bikers had managed to light a fire just far back enough from its mouth that it wouldn't attract attention. The walls reflected the heat, spreading it out further and making the place surprisingly warm. Bear was already taking advantage of that warmth, curled up and snoring in one corner. Ignatius was sitting close to the fire, keeping warm.

"You said that you would tell us your story once we were safe," Luna said, moving to sit down near him. "I don't know if there's anywhere safe, but there aren't actually monsters chasing us right now."

"So it's time to talk," Cub said. Luna saw Ignatius flinch at that.

"There's no need to be afraid of us," Luna said.

"You say that," he replied. "I don't think you would be so quick to do so if you knew about my past. Let's just say that I did some... not very pleasant things before the aliens came."

"Let's *not* just say it," Cub said. "How about you tell us exactly what you used to do, so my dad and I can decide how much of a threat you are to the club."

"Cub..." Luna began.

Cub shook his head, then looked around pointedly at the other people there in the storm drain, working to make the place into a temporary camp.

"I have to think about everyone else here too, Luna," he said, "and there's something off about a guy who can bring people back from being controlled by the aliens, who then talks about all the bad things he used to do. So what was it, Ignatius?"

"I... used to work for some people," he said. "They had me custom making compounds for them in a... private lab."

"You worked for drug dealers," Cub said, with a hard look. Luna looked across to Ignatius, feeling just as disgusted by the idea.

"It wasn't quite like that," Ignatius said, putting his hands up. "Well... yes, I suppose it *was* like that. But it was entirely legal, probably, sort of. The people I worked for had me working on substances that would be technically legal, but would still have effects on the human body. I worked on stimulants, mood enhancers, performance enhancers, brain improving compounds..."

"You sound almost proud of it," Luna said. It was hard not to see Ignatius in a different light after what he'd just said. It was hard not to see him as something grubbier now, and a lot harder to trust.

"*You're* riding with bikers," he shot back. "Besides, the kind of people I used to work for... they didn't exactly take no for an answer."

"So how did you come up with a cure?" Luna demanded.

"I was working on this... well, it doesn't really matter what it was," Ignatius said. "Suffice it to say that it didn't work as planned. Yet, when all those around me were transforming, I was left unchanged. I realized that I had something that might be able to help the world!"

"And you didn't try to sell it to people?" Luna said. "You just went out and started helping people?"

"I helped *you*, didn't I?" he retorted. "There's no need to be ungrateful. I'm not such an unpleasant person. I just…"

He didn't finish that sentence, because he was busy staring over Luna's shoulder. Bobby was growling again and Luna looked round and saw Bear standing there, big and silent, moving jerkily. By the firelight, Luna could see the pure white of his pupils.

"Dad…" Cub began, standing up, but Bear swatted him aside one-handed, sending him flying.

Luna was in his path next, and she barely had enough time to stand up before Bear grabbed for her, meaty hands fastening onto her neck. Luna felt her throat close off as the big biker's hands tightened around it, stopping all air from getting through to her lungs.

She kicked out at him, connecting with his knees, then his groin. None of it seemed to make a difference. She'd felt for herself the controlled people's indifference to pain, and even if he hadn't been controlled, Luna could never have fought a man the size of Bear and won. It didn't stop her trying, though. Bobby bit at the biker, and Bear sent him flying.

"Dad, you have to fight this," Cub said, scrambling back into the fight. "All of you, help me to get him off her!"

The other bikers lunged forward, grabbing at Bear and trying to pull him back. Luna got a breath of air as his grip broke for a moment, but that was only so that he could punch another of the bikers, knocking him flat. One hit him with a club hard enough to break it, but it made no difference. Bear fastened his hands onto Luna's throat again, and the world closed in around her.

"Dad!" Cub said. He had a machete in his hand now. Luna could see how that hand was shaking. "You have to let her go! You're going to kill Luna!"

The world was starting to go black, but still Bear wasn't letting go. Cub hit him, slicing at his arm. With any normal person, it would have made them let go, and probably left them in screaming in agony too. Bear wasn't a normal person anymore, though. Luna just felt the pressure on her throat continue, powerless to stop it.

"I'm sorry," Cub said. "I'm sorry, Dad."

Luna wanted to scream to him not to do it as he lifted the machete, but she didn't have any breath with which to do it. She could only watch as Cub swept the blade down, hacking through his father's neck, striking once, then again as he tried to cut through.

Above Luna, Bear went still, tumbling down to the floor as his grip broke away from her throat. Luna coughed, rubbing at her neck

47

and sucking in air as fast as she could. She could see Cub there, staring down at the weapon in his hands, staggering back.

"What have I done?" he murmured. "What have I *done*?"

"I would say that you saved the young lady, and possibly all of us," Ignatius said. "With one of the controlled that size—"

"He was my father!" Cub roared, and took a step forward, lifting the machete. "You did this! You said that you'd cured us, but you didn't do anything for him! You're just a mangy, drug-making cockroach!"

Luna managed to put herself between the two, lifting a hand to Cub's chest. "Cub, don't. It's not Ignatius's fault. It's the aliens'."

She could see the tears streaming from Cub's eyes, and the only thing Luna could think to do was what he had done for her. She hugged him, holding onto him while he cried.

"My dad... he was going to... I couldn't let him. I knew he'd rather die than turn into a murderer. And now *I'm* a murderer!"

"You're the person who just saved me," Luna said, "and you stopped your father from being a prisoner inside his own body. You did the only thing you could."

"I..." Cub began. Luna heard the machete clatter to the ground. "I need to get some air. I can't see him like this... I can't..."

He pulled back from Luna and ran out. Luna wanted to run after him, but she felt as though she could barely stand right then, let alone follow him.

"Go with him," she said instead to a couple of the bikers. "Make sure nothing happens to him. You and you, move Bear's body. It shouldn't be here when Cub comes back."

It felt weird, giving instructions to adults like that. It felt even weirder that they obeyed, doing what she asked and looking grateful that *someone* was giving them instructions. Maybe it was just gratitude that someone knew what to do next. Luna wished someone would tell *her*.

For now, she sat down opposite Ignatius. Bobby came to her, curling up against her, licking her hand.

"He was going to kill me," the man said.

"He still might," Luna said. "When Cub comes back in, he's going to want answers. We'll *all* want answers. Why didn't the cure work?"

Ignatius shook his head. "I don't know. It was never designed for this. It worked as a vaccine, so I hoped it might work as a cure, but obviously once someone has been controlled the effects aren't as permanent. Maybe it's something to do with—"

"Are you telling me that it will wear off for all of us?" Luna demanded. "How soon?"

"I don't know," Ignatius said. "I'm just—"

"Right now you have a choice," Luna said. "You can try to run and hope that Cub doesn't get hold of you, or you can give us all some answers. So how long?"

Ignatius went quiet, pursing his lips. He started to do some calculations on his fingers. "Assuming a steady rate of decay, and if I'm able to dose you all again at regular intervals, which means grabbing more of the formula from my truck…"

"How long?" Luna repeated.

"A week," Ignatius said. "A week at the very most. Obviously, that's a very rough calculation though. Some people would turn sooner."

A week. Luna sat there in silence, staring at the man she thought had saved them all. A week wasn't enough time. A week was barely enough to do anything, and certainly not long enough to be the rest of her life as something human.

"How do we extend that?" she asked, when she was able to form the words. "How do we make this into a real cure?"

"We don't," Ignatius said.

"That's not a good enough answer," Luna replied. "You found this, and you obviously have *some* skills, so what do we do?"

"I don't *know*," Ignatius insisted. "Maybe we could find some way to extend things, but I'm out of my depth. I would need to talk to other scientists, and try to find out why this has been only a temporary cure, but I don't even know where there are other *people*, let alone ones with the skills to help."

Luna found herself thinking about the Survivors then. She and the others had left them behind in LA. They'd been able to help with finding the virus to attack the aliens. Maybe they could help with this, especially when they'd been some of the first to mention rumors of a cure.

It felt like a long shot. It felt like the kind of thing that could never work, even if the Survivors were still okay. Yet what was the alternative? Luna looked across to where two of the bikers were still dragging out Bear's body, managing to move it only a little at a time across the concrete floor. *That* was the alternative. In maybe a week, that would be her. That would be all of them.

"In the morning we're going to LA," Luna said. "I think you'd better hope that we find what we need there."

49

CHAPTER EIGHT

Kevin followed Purest Xan as the alien led him through the spire once more. Curiously, he still found himself thinking about Chloe. Mostly, he found himself wondering how he had ever felt anything about her. Feeling things for someone felt like such a weakness, such an *aberration*, that it was hard to believe he had ever been like this.

"The longer you are with the Hive, the harder such foolishness will be to believe," Purest Xan said as they moved through the spire's levels. "Residue of a former life is common for those who are brought into the Hive, but it will fade."

"That's good to hear," Kevin said. For a moment he'd been worried that these memories of feelings would be with him forever. He was pretty sure that memories of someone who was soon to be reshaped for the good of the Hive would become annoying after a while.

He frowned slightly at that thought.

"Purest Xan," he asked, "do you ever worry that in not feeling things, we might be missing out on something?"

Purest Xan stopped. "You must be wary of saying such things, Kevin. In the Hive, any yearning for the times before we scoured ourselves of emotion is reckoned a kind of rebellion, a crime of the highest order."

"Why, Purest Xan?" Kevin asked. "Doesn't being cut off from emotions stop us from feeling happy, or from loving each other?"

"Such things are traps," Purest Xan said. "Our emotions were a part of what caused us to destroy our world's surface, so long ago. A creature will do foolish things to feel happy; things that are not for the good of the Hive. To yearn for such things is to yearn for separation from the whole."

"But—"

"That is enough, Kevin," Purest Xan said. "The thing you are talking about is not something that is discussed. Ever."

"I'm sorry," Kevin said. "I didn't know."

"That is why I have answered your questions before we arrive," Purest Xan said.

That caught Kevin's curiosity. "Arrive where?"

"In the Hall of Communion. Come."

The alien continued to lead the way, stepping into a kind of egg-shaped capsule. Kevin stepped in alongside the alien, waiting as the door sealed closed, seeming to grow over the gap. He stood still beside Purest Xan, waiting.

There was a brief sensation of movement, and although the walls of the capsule seemed to insulate them from it in a way that the floating platform before would not have, Kevin had the feeling that it moved far faster, shooting across to some distant point of the world ship before coming to a halt.

"Welcome to our Hall of Communion," Purest Xan said, as the door dissolved. "You should be honored. It is rare for one who is not of the Purest to be allowed here."

"I am honored," Kevin said. He knew that his place in the Hive was not quite that of the Purest. He had seen it in the moment of connection to it. "But... why have you brought me here?"

"You will see, Kevin," Purest Xan said.

They stepped out of the capsule and for a moment, all Kevin could do was stand and marvel. They stood on a platform that floated at the very center of a sphere of the same golden metal that the spires were constructed from. Other members of the Purest stood there, reflected in the shine of the golden metal, so that it was briefly difficult to tell how many there were. Counting, Kevin realized that there couldn't have been more than a hundred or so.

"Is this... the Purest's government or something?" Kevin asked.

"This is all of us, Kevin," Purest Xan said. "All of our station who travel on this world ship."

It took Kevin a second to really understand what the alien meant.

"These are all of the Purest?"

"There are others on other ships, and on the home world, but yes," Purest Xan said.

Kevin found it hard to imagine. There were so many aliens aboard the world ship, and the ship itself was so vast, that it seemed impossible that there should be only these few of their leaders. It seemed impossible that there should be world after world plundered for the benefit of just a tiny number of creatures.

He thought of the golden spires throughout the world ship. Judging by the number of the Purest here, there couldn't be more than a handful in each spire. Each was like a mansion, sticking out from the rest of the world ship, supporting two or three of the creatures at a time.

"Step forward, Kevin," one of the others said. A glance into the shared mind of the Hive told Kevin that its name was Purest Lux.

Kevin moved forward to the center of the platform, the aliens walking around him as if examining him. He wondered what they might be looking for that they hadn't already seen when they had gone through his mind. He tried to make out Purest Xan, but in the whirl of them it was difficult to pick out the alien.

"You are wondering what you are doing here, Kevin," Purest Lux said.

"Yes," Kevin admitted. He looked around him. "With all of this, and all the things I've seen, I don't understand what use I can be to the Hive."

The aliens could do things he'd only dreamed of, had managed to conquer his entire planet with ease, and had been clever enough to manipulate him into doing everything they wanted. How could he possibly be useful to things like that?

"You underestimate yourself," Purest Lux said. "We believe that you can be very useful to the Hive. When we sent our signals to your planet, there were those who tried to warn you. We plan to use you to locate them. After that, you will help us to move on to new planets, making it easier to gather resources for our home world."

Both of those sounded like worthy goals to Kevin, goals that would let him be of great use to the Hive. Truthfully, that was all he wanted now. Even so, it was hard to believe that he would really be able to do all that the Purest hoped.

"How am I going to do it?" he asked. "I mean... why me, I guess."

"Your brain can do all that we require of it," Purest Lux said. "It can connect to those we seek, and we will follow that signal. It can decipher their attempts to hide. It can unlock whatever protections they have in place. Beyond that, worlds might trust an unknown child-thing where they might not trust us. You are our emissary, Kevin. You will find the path for us and pave the way for conquest."

"Yes, Purest Lux," Kevin said.

Dimly, he was aware that there had been a time when he would have recoiled from everything the alien had just said. Just a short time ago, he would have refused to be a part of something like this, and would have seen anyone opposing the Hive as good creatures, to be protected. Even days ago, he would have said that he would rather die than be involved in something like this.

It all seemed so foolish now. Why wouldn't he help the Hive? Its well-being was the only measure of what was good in the universe. To try to stand against it was the very definition of evil. Kevin could hardly believe all the strange ways that he'd thought until they'd made him a part of that wonderful, interconnected web of light.

"What do I need to do?" Kevin asked.

"For now, stand where you are," Purest Lux said.

The curving walls around Kevin shifted now, making it seem that he was standing in the middle of space, in a spot that was nowhere even close to the Earth. He could make out a double star burning brightly above him, larger than the sun, while planets spun in orbit around them. There was a gap in those orbits, marked by a field of debris, and somehow Kevin knew this was the spot where the aliens' planet had been. They'd burned it to try to save themselves, and it still hadn't been enough to stop the Hive from ripping their planet apart for everything it held.

One of the Purest came forward, attaching a series of shell-like buds to Kevin's head. Now, each time he turned his head, the room seemed to turn with him. He was a part of the world ship, and its systems were linked to everything he saw.

"Reach out, Kevin," Purest Lux said. "Immerse yourself in the Hive, and at the same time reach out for the feeling that you had when you received messages from the ones who fled the fall of their world."

Kevin did his best. Delving into the Hive was the easy part; that was waiting for him the moment he wanted it, in an all-consuming connection that seemed to fill every corner of his being.

The connection to the aliens that had contacted him was harder. He had never sought them out before, never managed to connect without a signal coming to him. It had never even felt like it might be something in his control. Instead, it had always come on their terms and their schedule. Only the thought that he was doing this for the good of the Hive made Kevin keep going.

He thought about what it had been like the first time a vision had come to him, the numbers burning across his brain. He thought about what it had been like when the signal had come through to try to warn him about the Hive, about how it had felt, about the way the connection had poured into his brain…

He felt the moment when his mind made the link, tasting the scent of the aliens' signals like a bloodhound picking out a familiar smell.

"There!" he said, pointing, but he didn't need to point because the world ship was already moving. Kevin saw space bending around the vessel, and more than that, he felt it. He felt the ripples and eddies in space that the world ship's drives caused, felt the way it bent space around itself to cross vast distances. To Kevin, it seemed like surfing on a tide composed of the galaxy's great forces: the heat of stars and the pull of gravity, the spin of atoms and the radiating waves of light.

He shouldn't have known how to guide a world ship across all of that, but, linked into the Hive, he did. He followed the scent of the aliens who had fled from the devastation of their world, tracking it in ways that were all about instinct. He clung to it, refusing to let go, letting his mind lead the world ship through the blackness of space.

It didn't hurt. Ordinarily, it was hard, even painful, to cling onto this kind of connection. Just translating signals made his brain ache normally, and threatened to send Kevin blacking out into a seizure. Now, he was doing something that should have been a hundred times harder, and he felt nothing.

It was just one of the ways that the Hive had made him stronger.

He blinked, and now the stars around the world ship were stationary once again. One lay closer than the others, pale and small; a tiny, worn out thing that seemed to barely declare its presence against the dark. A solitary planet circled it, looking blue and life filled in spite of its star's small size. Kevin stared out at it, seeing the oceans and the continents there, the small moons circling it and the satellites that lay in orbit.

"There," he said. "The aliens who contacted me are there."

He could feel their presence if he tried, picking out their signals on the edge of his consciousness. Kevin's connection to the Hive let him turn listening devices toward the planet, feeding in those signals so that his brain could translate them.

"They know we're here," he said. "They know we've found them."

"Let them know," Purest Lux said. "It changes nothing."

Kevin listened to the signals, hearing the panic and the fear. There were signals from military figures trying to find a way to defend the world and signals from families trying to think of a way to flee it. Once, he had thought that these aliens sounded so much warmer compared to the Hive. Now, they just sounded weak to him.

"They are getting ready to fight or run," Kevin told the others. He looked down at the planet, seeing its swirling clouds and the faint dots of cities down on the surface. He'd seen the world ship's factories and forges, ready to take apart anything brought to them. How much would they find down there? How much would they be able to take from this fresh world that Kevin had been able to find for them?

"What do we do now?" Kevin asked, expecting to hear the details of the invasion. He had no doubt that the world ship could capture somewhere like this easily.

"Now," Purest Lux said, "we destroy it."

CHAPTER NINE

Luna woke to the sound of snuffling and whining. For a moment, she thought it was some strange dream, and that eventually it would change into the sound of her mother trying to wake her up because she was going to be late for school.

Then she remembered that her school, and her mother, and just about everything else on Earth, was gone, and the sheer pain of that thought was enough to propel her into wakefulness, her eyes snapping open to take in the interior of the storm drains, the morning light coming in at their edge.

She saw the coyotes there, yapping and dragging something, their mouths bloody. It took her a moment to realize what was going on.

"Coyotes! They've got Bear's body!"

She ran forward, trying to scare them off, because she'd heard somewhere that coyotes were usually pretty frightened of people. That might have been the case normally, but maybe the end of the human world had made them bolder, or maybe they were just too hungry to leave a potential meal alone, because they growled and snarled at her, one snapping at her hand.

The pain as it bit her was excruciating, and Luna jerked back, which only made it worse. The bikers were coming forward now, striking at the coyotes with whatever weapons they had, clubs and knives rising and falling. Cub was at their heart, kicking at one of the coyotes to try to make it back away. Luna saw it twist toward him, biting his leg just as it had bitten her hand. She saw Cub wince, but he didn't cry out. Instead, he struck down at the coyote, and Luna waded in, adding her own kick aimed at the side of one of the creatures.

Finally the coyotes turned and ran, obviously realizing that there were too many humans to take on. Luna saw Cub turn toward the remains of his father, looking horrified by what the coyotes had done. She pulled him back as gently as she could.

"You shouldn't look," she said. She didn't want to look either, but somehow, it seemed wrong to look away. This felt like a world now where they didn't get the luxury of ignoring the things that were wrong.

"We need to bury him," Cub said. "We don't have time but..."
He rounded on the other bikers, and although plenty of them were

56

older than him, they still flinched back. "You were supposed to take him deep into the tunnels where this couldn't happen!"

"It's not their fault," Luna said. "It's not anybody's fault except the aliens'. If they hadn't come, then none of this would have happened. There's nothing they could have done. Nothing *you* could have done."

That was the lesson that this world seemed to have for them now: that sometimes it didn't matter what they did; bad things would happen anyway. To Luna, it seemed like a really harsh lesson to have to learn at their age. It seemed more like the kind of thing to put off learning as long as possible, or even ignore completely.

"I will ignore it," Luna told herself.

"What?" Cub said.

Luna shook her head. "Nothing."

She would though. She wasn't going to accept that there was nothing she could do about the world. If she really believed that, then she might as well sit down, wait for a week, and fade back into control by the aliens. She had to think that there was something they could do if only they got to LA.

Luna knew they weren't going to be able to go anywhere until they'd buried Bear, though. They might only have a week, and that was assuming that they could get the rest of Ignatius's vaccine, but she wasn't going to argue about whether they had enough time for this. Looking at Cub's face, she knew that no one was.

***

They buried Bear as deep as they could in the hard, rocky ground. Luna took her turn with the digging, although now she didn't have the strength or the immunity to pain that had made it so easy to do the heavy work of pulling Sedona apart before. Cub kept working until Luna pulled him back, knowing that he would probably work until he dropped in the heat.

"Let the others finish the digging," she said, as Ignatius and the bikers kept going. The man who had saved them seemed to be working as hard as anyone, as if hoping it would make up for his failure to come up with a more permanent solution.

"He's my dad," Cub said.

"That's why you should think of something to say about him," Luna said.

"Me? I'm just—"

"I'm pretty sure you're in charge now," Luna said. When Cub had started giving orders last night, the bikers had done everything he said, in spite of him being only a little older than her. She reached out to take his hand. "I know it hurts. My parents aren't dead, but I don't know where they are, and when I realized that they'd been transformed..."

She half expected Cub to say that it wasn't the same, and she guessed that it wasn't. They had hope now that there might be a way to change people back, and maybe that meant that she would see her parents again, and everything would be okay, and...

No, things would never be the same as they were.

"I don't know if I can do it," Cub said. "I don't know if I can stand there and just say goodbye."

"I'll be there with you," Luna promised him. "It doesn't have to be much, but I think it will be better if you say something. I think you'll regret it if you don't."

"I'll try," Cub said.

They waited there for the bikers to finish the grave, lowering Bear's body into it carefully, with the kind of reverence that said that they were all hurting doing it. Most of them looked drawn, and like they were holding back tears, trying to be tough even though their leader was gone.

Cub looked at Luna as though her hand on his arm was the only reason he was able to get up in front of them. She hoped he would be able to do this. Most of the world hadn't had the chance to say goodbye to anyone; it felt right that he should, at least.

"I don't really know what to say," he said while Luna stood beside him. "My dad... you all knew what he was like. He was the strongest person I ever knew, and the toughest, but he always tried to do the right thing. He taught me... he taught me just about everything," Cub managed, and to Luna, it felt as though he was about to break down, but maybe that wasn't a bad thing. Maybe they all needed time to mourn.

Luna found herself thinking about Bear and the help that he'd given them, but she also found herself thinking about Kevin and Chloe, about her family, and about everyone else they'd lost. In that moment, she didn't let tears fall only for the big man who had helped them to get through to the alien ships; she cried for the whole world that was gone.

She and Cub stood there while the others filled in the grave. It wasn't the kind of funeral that was normal, but maybe it was the kind of thing that was right for now. Luna wasn't sure what she could say to Cub that might make it any better, so she just put an arm around him and stood there while the bikers and Ignatius put back the red earth and leveled off the ground.

They stood there for what seemed like the longest time, and although Luna didn't want to be the one to force them to go, she knew that she would need to be. The other bikers all had too much respect for Bear, Cub obviously didn't want to leave his father's grave, and Ignatius wouldn't want to risk saying anything when the others already disliked him. That left Luna.

"We need to go," she said, gently.

Cub looked over at her.

"I'm sorry," she said. "But we have to. We only have a week."

Cub was quiet for a moment or two, but then nodded.

"You're right," he said. He looked out to the others, raising his voice. "We have to go. Get your stuff. We need to start walking."

***

They set off walking, trudging together in the direction of LA, and Luna could feel the heat beating down on her with every step. They kept Sedona at their backs, not daring to go toward it.

"I wish we'd been able to get the bikes," Cub said, as the other bikers marched along in a long line.

"If the aliens are looking for us anywhere, it will be in Sedona," Ignatius replied. "Besides, my stash of vaccine is more important."

"If it works," Cub snapped.

Luna put a hand on his arm, keeping the peace. She didn't like Ignatius much more than anyone else, but at least he'd done his best to save them, risking himself to do it. That had to count for something.

"The energy blasts probably mean the bikes aren't even there," she said.

"Yeah," Cub said, looking downcast. It occurred to Luna just how much those bikes probably meant to them.

"How much further to where you left the vaccine, Ignatius?" Luna asked, trying to distract Cub.

"Not far," he said. "I put it in an old scrapyard where I would find it. Of course, I counted on being able to just *drive* back to it, rather than having to walk through a desert."

"Stop complaining," Cub said.

They kept walking, the heat of the day growing around them. Luna was sweating already, and she wanted something to drink almost more than anything in the world. Almost; she would have taken Kevin and Chloe coming back ahead of any of it.

59

They slowed as the heat grew, the effort of walking making it seem as if they wouldn't be able to keep going much longer. Luna felt as though she had to concentrate just to keep putting one foot in front of the other. Much more of this and they would have to stop. They would *have* to.

"There," Ignatius said, pointing.

Luna saw the shine of metal in the distance, although on second glance it wasn't very shiny. She could see the colors of rust and dust, metal stacked on top of metal in mound after mound, a scrapyard just sitting there behind a chain-link fence.

The sight of it was enough to draw them on, making them hurry forward. It was far enough from the city that it still seemed untouched by the aliens, left silent and still in the desert heat. It seemed like only a short time before they reached the chain-link fence there, large signs proclaiming the consequences for anyone who trespassed.

"There's no one here," Ignatius said. "I checked."

He led the way inside, opening a gate where the chain holding it shut had been cut open. Luna guessed that he'd been the one to do it. He led the way through the scrapyard to a spot where a metal plate stood at the side of a pile of rusted metal pipes. He pulled it away, coming out with a large ice box, from which he started to take vials of blue liquid.

"Here," Ignatius said, tossing one to Luna. "Drink this."

Luna caught it, opening it carefully. "This is the vaccine?"

"We'll see if drinking it helps concentrate the dose."

Luna didn't like the idea that Ignatius didn't know what it would do. Even so, she drank it slowly, ignoring the horrible taste as best she could. Ignatius passed around more of the vaccine to the others and they drank it, not looking happy about it.

"It's going to be a long way to LA, walking and drinking that," Cub said.

"Maybe we should look round the scrapyard," Luna suggested, "see if there's anything we can use."

"There isn't anything," Ignatius insisted. "I took all the food and water the first time, and the cars are all broken."

"*How* broken?" Cub asked, in a thoughtful tone of voice.

"What are you thinking?" Luna asked. There was something about the way he'd asked it that made her hopeful.

"I'm thinking that pretty much everyone in this club has worked on cars and bikes. If we can find some tools, maybe some welding gear... Spread out," he ordered the others. "See what you can find. Luna, do you want to come with me?"

60

Luna nodded. "It's *definitely* a better idea than walking."

They started to look around the yard, seeing the piles of cars, the flattened wrecks, and the long-destroyed engines. The first piles weren't very promising, looking as though no one in the world would ever be able to get them running again.

Then they rounded one of the stacks and Luna saw it.

"It's perfect," she said, staring.

"If it will run," Cub said.

The school bus sat in the middle of it all, big and solid looking, intact except for some of the glass, and looking as though it was only a little way from running down the road.

"It might have problems with some of the cars in the way," Luna said.

Cub pointed to what looked like the front of an old snowplow, although why something like that was in a scrapyard in the middle of the desert, Luna couldn't imagine.

"We can fit that to the front," Cub said, "maybe take some panels and make some armor for the sides."

"We can make our own tank," Luna said with a smile. "I *like* it. If we can do it."

"We can do it," Cub promised. "Over here, everyone!"

The bikers came over, and plenty of them had found tools. One of them had a welding rig, while others had grinders and jacks, wrenches and hammers.

"I think whoever owned this liked to work on the better cars," one said. "What do you want us to do, Cub?"

Cub explained the plan, and if the bikers thought it was a lot, they didn't say anything. Instead, they swarmed over the bus, getting to work on rebuilding it and reshaping it. They grabbed parts from the scrap heap, cutting at them and placing them, finding ways to make them work. Luna got the feeling that they were happy to have something to do that would actually help.

Luna decided to join in, and even if she wasn't able to help rebuild parts of the engine or weld things together, she could find pieces of armor plate for it, and help the others to drag metal from the heaps.

Slowly, the bus came together. It looked like the kind of bus kids might have used to go to school in the middle of a war zone, armor covered and hardened against anything that might get in the way. Luna tried to ignore the time that it took to do it; it wasn't wasted, because once it was done, it would be far quicker than walking.

Even so, it seemed to take forever to come together, but slowly there was less and less to do, and more and more of the bikers stepped back from it. Finally, Cub stood in front of it, a broad smile on his face.

"Is it ready?" Luna asked.

Cub nodded, looking satisfied. "It's ready."

CHAPTER TEN

They made Chloe walk down to the flesh factories, ignoring her attempts to pull free of the large, armored hands that held her, treating her attempts to talk to them with contempt. Or maybe just not understanding; after all, the great transformed creatures that led her down there didn't exactly seem like the cleverest things that had ever been put together.

"Put together" was the right way to think about it, because as they made her walk down through the interior of the factories, she saw creatures literally being constructed, like models being built by some kid ready for painting. She saw a space where red hot armor was being pushed into place onto giant, hairless things that looked like bloated cousins to the Purest. In another spot, things with blades for hands grew in giant glass canisters.

"Where are you taking me?" Chloe demanded. "What are you planning to do with me?"

She tried not to let any of the terror she felt show in her voice. She wanted to be brave, and she *didn't* want to give these creatures the satisfaction of knowing just how much this place scared her. She'd learned a long time ago that for some people, seeing fear just meant that they treated you worse. When she'd run away, she'd learned not to show any weakness, and before that...

No, she wouldn't think about before that. It was even better to stare at the things going on around her than to think about the times before that. At least *this* was being done by actual monsters, not the kind who pretended to be nice, and normal, and kind in the moments when they weren't doing worse things.

So she stared at the horrors around her, refusing to look away, refusing to let them see the way it scared her. That wasn't easy, though, because there was something truly hellish about that place. There were benches with people and aliens strapped down, screaming as creatures ate their way out of their bodies, being born into the world through the carnage. There was a room where a lizard-like humanoid was pinned to a wall, and a pair of aliens were apparently cutting it open and then waiting while its body healed, faster than Chloe could have believed. There was another room where the only purpose of anything within seemed to be to cause pain, testing and retesting the limits of the people and creatures within.

63

"I know what you're doing!" Chloe said defiantly. "I know that you're trying to scare me, and it won't work!"

Then she saw the room with the chair in it, and she screamed.

"No! No, I won't let you take me there, I won't!"

The room ahead was broad and featureless at ground level except for a chair that reminded her of a dentist's chair: shining metal and obviously designed to recline flat if needed. There were no straps or restraints on it, but Chloe didn't let that fool her; she'd already felt how easily the Hive could use gravity itself to hold their victims in place.

Three of the Purest stood near the chair, dressed in long white outfits that reminded Chloe of doctors' coats. The blank, disinterested way they looked at her as their creatures brought her forward was bad enough. The rest of the room was worse.

Around the room, arranged in tiers that stretched upward, there were seats, so that the chair was at the center of a bull's-eye of them, allowing those in the seats to look down at everything that went on. More of the Purest sat in those seats, along with some of their lesser creatures, which hung back on the higher tiers, away from their rulers. Chloe had seen a picture of a Victorian dissecting theater once, where doctors had performed autopsies for people to watch and learn from. At the time, she had thought that it was creepy, but kind of cool. Now, it just seemed creepy.

"No," Chloe begged. "Please."

She fought as they dragged her forward, kicking out at the creatures who held her and trying to wrench herself free. She tried going limp, so that they would have to carry more of her weight, and tried calling out for help from anything nearby that wasn't completely in thrall to the Hive.

None of it made any difference. They lifted Chloe as easily as if she had been a feather, placing her in the chair and pinning her in place while one of the Purest used a device to adjust the gravity and hold her in place.

"I am Purest Ro," it said through a translator box. "These are Purest Gal and Purest Jir. You will be still and silent while we discuss the next step in your examination."

"I will not!" Chloe shouted back at the alien. "Let me go. Let me go, and give Kevin back to me the way he was. You'll pay for this, all of you."

She didn't know why she was making threats. Threatening people who were about to hurt you didn't work; it just made them hurt you worse. Even so, she wasn't just going to sit quietly and wait for them to start doing whatever it was they were planning to do to her next. She wasn't just going to sit there and be their victim, even if that meant that things were worse for her because of it.

The aliens started to engage in what Chloe guessed was a silent conversation, looking over to her from time to time in the same way that a butcher might look at a carcass, silently working out the best places to cut to get the most out of her. Chloe could only imagine what they were discussing. The best experiments to run on her, probably, and what order to run them in so that she would live as long as possible.

"I will not be scared," she told herself. "I will not be scared."

She wished Kevin were there. If he were there, he would find a way to pull her out of this chair, and they would run together. They would find a way to get out of here and back to Earth, even if they were somewhere else completely by now.

Except it had been Kevin who had sent her here, as blank and emotionless as the rest of them, acting as if he had never seen Chloe before in his life. The moment he'd woken up from the things the aliens had done, it had been as if he had been a completely different person. He'd walked out of the room as if she hadn't even been there. When he'd come back, there had been that cruel edge to him that all of the aliens seemed to have, looking at her as if she were nothing, not seeming like the Kevin she knew at all.

"Your mind is quite interesting," Purest Ro said to her, taking out some of the small, tentacled things that they'd used before to examine her brain. "Even for one of your kind, it seems filled with the heresy of emotions. It has been decided that we will explore this first, before we begin to implant and augment you. We will explore your reactions to agony, of course, and to different emotional states, to see how far you can be pushed before your brain shuts down."

It said it in the same tones it might have used if it were proposing some small, painless process, rather than her slow murder over however long the aliens could make her last.

"Remain as still as possible," Purest Ro said, starting to stick the tiny, tentacled things into place. "We wish to make the placement as precise as possible."

Of course, Chloe did her best to move out of the way. She wasn't going to make this easy for them, wasn't going to give them *anything* that they wanted if she had a chance to fight back.

They gave her no chance, though. Purest Ro fastened the things to her skull, and then the Hive was buzzing through her mind once more.

Chloe tried to push them out, and it hurt. It hurt like a thousand glass shards cutting into her brain, each one made of light and snagging at her memories. She found them pulling at the memories of her time as a runaway, forcing images into her mind of time spent in doorways and under bridges, in abandoned buildings and in any corner she could find where the more predatory people on the streets wouldn't find her.

Each memory seemed to carry with it an entire cargo of emotions. The image of an old woman, still in a doorway, and the moment Chloe realized she wasn't breathing, brought with it a sense of sorrow and loss. Glimpses of social services and cops from between the slats of a stack of pallets brought fear and a determination never to be taken back.

That thought was a betrayal, telling them exactly where to go to hurt her most. It brought with it images of the past that she'd tried to run away from: the arguments with the mother who wouldn't believe her, and who called her a liar. The father who was perfect whenever he was out in the world, and whose face turned to something far angrier, far uglier, the moment the doors were safely shut. Chloe's memories threw up fragments of sensation, each one bringing with it far too much to cope with: the weight of someone on top of her, the whispered threats if she should tell someone, the pain of the knife the times she tried to make it stop…

"No," she told herself, told *them*. "I won't think about it all. You can't *make* me."

They'd called her crazy, called her borderline, made her go to see therapists and put her on so many different medications that it was hard to keep track of them all. Chloe had learned *some* skills from it, even if they weren't always the ones that they'd meant to teach her. She hadn't learned how to control everything she felt, but she had learned how to hide emotions away, and pretend that she wasn't feeling things… and to use them like weapons.

Ordinarily, it was just about using words. Chloe was good at seeing the emotions in other people, and saying exactly the right, or wrong, thing. She'd done it too much with Luna, she knew, because it was obvious that she liked Kevin, even if Kevin didn't seem to see it. Now, though, she took her emotions and she started to ball them up inside herself, stretch them out, shaping them like an arrowhead, or a knife.

Chloe focused on thoughts of Kevin for a moment, thinking about how much she cared about him, and how special he was. Those thoughts were like a safe space in which she could gather herself up, and avoid the worst that the aliens could throw at her. Chloe was good at using thoughts like that to pull back from the world and ignore the worst things that might be happening in it.

"Not today," she told herself. "Today, they're going to hurt for it."

Chloe dove back into the stream of minds trying to mess with hers, and she plunged her emotions into them, striking out with them like the weapon they were. These were minds that hadn't experienced emotions firsthand, after all, and Chloe found her emotions hard enough to deal with even after a lifetime of doing so. She cut and hacked with anger, threw fear over their minds like a net, and hardened love until it became something to plunge straight into a heart, rather than something that seemed to fill it up to the brim.

"This is *my* mind!" she yelled at them. "Not yours, *mine!*"

She lashed out at them, cutting at the links to her, and at the links between them, slashing them like they were an old pair of jeans ready to be made into cut-offs. She attacked because anything was better than not doing it, because she *refused* to sit there quietly, whatever they threatened to—

One of them reached into whatever part of Chloe's brain was responsible for pain, and it *squeezed.*

Chloe screamed as she came back to herself, sobbing with the agony of it even when the member of the Purest let go of its grip on her mind. One of them stood, moving forward, and somehow Chloe knew this had been the one to hurt her like that. It had a look of satisfaction, as if it had almost *enjoyed* doing it.

"That is enough," the alien said. "This is foolishness, caring about *emotions.*"

"Yes, Purest Lux," Purest Ro said, bowing its head in acquiescence.

"There is nothing to be learned from pursuing such a thing," Purest Lux continued, "and it comes dangerously close to breaking our most important strictures. The emotions of lesser beings are a contamination, not a toy to examine."

"You are correct, of course, Purest Lux," Purest Ro said.

"We must act in the way that is best for the Hive," Purest Lux continued. "This... creature is too contaminated with emotion to work with its mind, but its flesh may still be of use. What are your plans for the next stages of processing it?"

"We believe that it is a suitable candidate to test the interactions of implants on," Purest Ro said. "After that, Purest Jir and Purest Gal have suggested either dissection or use as a host for one of the species that must be grown."

Chloe thought of the creatures that had burst out of aliens in one of the first rooms she'd seen. They were talking about using her as a combination of incubator and first meal for monsters!

"You disagree?" Purest Lux asked.

"Since the human will be partly changed by any implants, would there not be benefit in transforming it completely?" Purest Ro asked.

Purest Lux stood there for several seconds, considering Chloe. "This creature is too uncontrolled to be of use. It could not be commanded to the Hive's satisfaction. Test what processes you wish on it, but then give it over to be devoured. There are plenty more humans where it came from, after all."

"Yes, Purest Lux," Purest Ro said, and again, Chloe had the sense of deference there. "Your wisdom benefits the Hive."

Purest Lux ignored the comment, turning to Chloe and staring at her. Chloe had the sense there of hatred on a level that had nothing to do with ordinary human ideas of it, or even the kind of hatred that she felt for all of them right then. This was a hatred that wouldn't even call itself that. It simply saw any life that was not like itself as an inconvenience, an obstruction to be removed. It was the kind of enemy that couldn't be talked to or reasoned with.

Worse, it was one who had decided that Chloe needed to die.

CHAPTER ELEVEN

Purest Ro kept pace with Chloe as they took her through from the viewing chamber into one of the implantation spaces and prepared to experiment on the human female further. Most of its fellow Purest didn't follow; apparently, looking inside her mind had been more than enough for them, without looking at the procedures that would follow.

Oddly, Purest Ro found itself thinking that perhaps it would be better for it not to be a part of those procedures either, and not just because of the fury that still punctuated Chloe's fear and horror as she glared out at them. There was the duty to the Hive to consider, and Purest Ro could not neglect the things that had to be done in its name.

"Place the human in a holding field," Purest Jir said, as they reached the implantation chamber.

This was one of the more advanced applications of the technology that the Hive had stolen from their neighbors so long ago. It was odd, Purest Ro thought, that it should think of it like that, when all knew that the Hive had the right to take everything that would make it stronger. Why else would other things be in the universe, after all?

The servitor creatures lifted Chloe into a spot in the middle of the room, and now, instead of pinning her in place, the gravity caught her in direction after direction, sending her tumbling so that no one way was down for more than a fraction of a second. It meant that she hung in the air, unable to act.

There was something, Purest Ro realized, both elegant and somewhat cruel about that.

"With which devices should we begin?" Purest Gal asked.

"Perhaps a bonded symbiont?" Purest Jir suggested.

"Or a graft," Purest Gal said. It picked up a metal replacement for a humanoid arm, clearly far too big. "What percentage of replacement do you think that human's form would tolerate?"

"No!" Purest Ro exclaimed, but then caught itself. "That is, that seems like an inefficient way of going about this. It would be difficult to return the human to an unaltered state for further experimentation after removing its limbs."

69

"That makes sense, Purest Ro," Purest Jir said. It picked up a silvery creature, ignoring the way its form shifted and thrashed, seeking flesh. "So, a joining then."

The three of them moved toward Chloe, who took one look at the thing in Purest Jir's hands and screamed, her terror obvious. It made no hint of difference to the others, but Purest Ro found itself... troubled by the idea that the young human should experience so much fear.

There was nothing it could do to alleviate that fear as the others pressed the symbiont to Chloe's arm, the inner teeth of the living metal creature biting down into her and making her scream again.

"Note the nuances of human screams," Purest Gal said. "Perhaps I will produce a knowledge collection on their various types."

Ro's fellow Purest said that as if the screams meant no more than the trilling of Xatha bats in the eaves of the counter-spin warehouses. Could they not see that this meant that Chloe was in pain, and that she would give anything for it to stop? It took an effort of will for Ro not to step forward and rip the device from Chloe's arm. Only the knowledge that doing so would harm her far more at this point stopped it.

"Now the first serum," Purest Gal said, pressing a syringe into Chloe before Ro could even think to stop it. She cried out again, and Ro winced in sympathy.

"This serum is a mutagenic one," Purest Gal explained. "The effects are somewhat unpredictable, but if it produces usable results..."

"They could be bred into a new servitor species," Purest Jir finished. "What else should we do with it? I still say that a metal graft would—"

"No," Ro said, firmly. When the others looked around, it realized that it had spoken too loudly once more, and thought quickly. "We are meant to be scientists, not merc... tinkerers. Already, we have two processes progressing in the human. Introduce more before we observe the results and it will be impossible to know what causes the results we get."

"I suppose you are correct," Purest Jir said. "Perhaps then we should leave the human for a while and see what changes the serum bring? Then we can decide on what to try next. I will tell you now, I will be arguing for metal grafts."

"We should base our next moves on the evidence," Ro said.

They left, and Ro found it curiously difficult to simply walk away from the human without looking back at her, spinning helplessly in a web of gravity. In the past, it had had no difficulties with performing even the most difficult and complex of procedures on subjects, yet today, two relatively simple things had it concerned about the subject's safety.

It was odd.

To try to remind itself that this was just one more experiment among many, Ro set out among the other stations, looking at other subjects, listening to the way they responded to the experiments… to their screams.

"What is happening to me?" Ro asked, recoiling from a room where subjects were slowly being farmed for bacteria, held in place while a range of diseases were bred inside their forms.

The next room was one where they were testing the training responses of subjects from different species, trying to find methods that would make them more useful as servants than the complete control used when they first took a planet. The screams from inside that room made Ro unwilling to even look into it.

There was room after room there, with experiments that Ro had helped to run, testing everything from physical transformation to the spliced breeding of new creatures and simply the testing to destruction of some of their creations. In one pit, two giant, spider-like creatures that looked like variants on the same genetic pattern fought so that the Purest above could determine which combination of genetic tweaks would prove superior. Ro turned away from it as quickly as the rest.

Purest Ro felt… well, that was just the issue. It *felt*, and not just the pure harmony that came from being a part of the Hive. It felt disgust, and fear, and horror. It felt sadness every time it heard a scream, and that was almost impossible to understand. Before, its connection to the Hive had let it reach into the minds of everything linked to it, but it hadn't found emotions there, because the Hive eliminated such weaknesses. Now, it was as if Ro could imagine what others must be feeling and reacted to it instinctively. Was this… empathy?

Empathy. Just one of a great many forbidden concepts, cast down as the things that had caused the wars among their people so long ago. Emotions were dangerous. Emotions caused conflicts among the Purest. Emotions were…

…overwhelming.

Was this what the human, Chloe, felt like all the time? No, that couldn't be possible. How could anyone contain so many layers of feelings without bursting apart? Ro had to walk away from the sentient experimental rooms, finding a quiet seating space among a

71

selection of hydroponically grown plants that were meant to be experiments in oxygen cultivation and food variation.

It was strange that Ro had never considered the beauty of it before. The golden spires and the restored spaces of the home world were beautiful, of course, but theirs was a beauty restored exactly as it had been, constructed mathematically, not because the Purest had a true, emotional appreciation of what that beauty meant.

Now, Ro looked at the beauty around it and wept. Not just from the beauty of it, although that was a part. There was so much more to it. There was the horror at what was going on in every corner. There was the roil of emotions long buried bubbling up inside Ro's head. There was a sense of guilt that threatened to overwhelm everything, forcing Ro to remember everything it had done... *he* had done. He was not an it, not some meaningless cog in a mechanism, but a living, breathing creature capable of making choices and feeling things for himself.

He felt so many things now; so very many.

Ro knew the moment when this had happened to him, down to the instant. It had not been some slow process of realization, or the kind of logical process of persuasion that the Hive preferred. It had happened in one moment inside Chloe's mind, when he had felt the emotions there, and she had used them like a weapon to lash out.

In that moment, she had cut at all of the Hive with the hardened knife of her emotions, yet it had been Ro who had been affected by it. Had that been because he had been the one deepest within her mind, and most vulnerable because of it? Had he merely been unfortunate to be in the way of what she had tried to do in order to break free? Or was there something about him that had been particularly susceptible? Was it some fundamental weakness inside him that had made him vulnerable to the poison of emotions?

Was there some cruel, traitorous part of him that had longed for disconnection from the Hive?

"Purest Ro, are you well?"

Ro looked up, composing himself in a hurry as he saw Purest Lux there. The Hive had no leaders, and no need for them when it operated by consensus, yet the more Ro thought about it, the more it seemed to him that often, that consensus seemed to follow the paths that Purest Lux suggested.

"Why do you ask, Purest Lux?" Ro asked, trying to buy some time in which to compose himself. Emotions were so *difficult*. They could not be marshalled and tidied away the way that pure, controlled thoughts could. Instead, they flew about inside him, untamable as *Grava* birds.

72

"You seem... out of balance," Purest Lux said. It wasn't quite a rebuke, wasn't quite a question, wasn't quite an accusation, but it felt far too close to all of those things for Ro's liking. "I am having trouble sensing you within the connection of the Hive."

"I am there," Ro said. It was true, as far as it went. He could still feel the Hive there, on the edge of his consciousness, but that wasn't the same thing as being a full part of it, enthralled in it in every sense.

Ro knew that he ought to explain exactly what was happening to him then. He ought to explain to Purest Lux about this sudden influx of feelings, and the sudden feeling of being disconnected from the whole. Of being an *individual*. He should confess to all of it, and hope that the others would have a way to wipe him clean of this contagion, reconnecting him with the Hive and purging all of this uncertainty from the interior of his being.

He didn't, though. He just sat and waited.

"Are you sure that there is nothing wrong?" Purest Lux said. "I would like to examine you to make sure that there has been no effect on you from all the things you have been working on recently."

Fear sprang up inside Ro. If Purest Lux saw what he was like... at the very least he would insist that Ro was changed back into what he was. At most... there might be accusations of treason, of trying to bring back forbidden things to the Hive. He might be destroyed for it, and while that should not have brought terror bubbling like flaws through rock, it did.

He couldn't deny the request either, though, because that would only *prove* that he was not a true part of the Hive. What did that leave?

"Purest Ro?" Purest Lux asked.

"Yes, of course," Purest Ro said. "Forgive me. I was distracted."

He tried to think, as quickly as possible. He found himself thinking, not of the Hive, but of Chloe. He found himself thinking of the way she compartmentalized things and hid them even from herself just to allow herself to function. He thought of the way that she found ways to ride the emotions that filled her and still function in the world.

Slowly, Ro began to build boxes within himself. He built them strong, and filled them with the emotions that he felt, hiding those boxes deep within the depths of his mind. He built a façade that was everything he could remember being within the Hive. Then he opened the outer layers of himself to Purest Lux.

73

He could feel the other member of the Purest looking around inside him like sentinel soldiers hunting around on a planet's surface for rebellious creatures or survivors. He guided the other around, and very carefully kept hidden those parts of himself that he knew would lead to his destruction.

It would not have worked if the Hive had been used to such things. If any of the Purest had turned to emotions at any point in as long as Ro could remember, perhaps Purest Lux would have known what to look for. It would not have worked if the Hive were used to its own kind lying to it.

It wasn't, though, and although Purest Lux stared at him for the longest time, eventually, it stepped back from Ro.

"Thank you, Purest Ro. It would seem that all is well in you."

"All is well in me," Purest Ro agreed.

"Very well," Purest Lux said. "We will await the results of your work with the human."

The Purest went away, leaving Ro alone with his thoughts, and he *was* alone. He could reach out and touch the Hive if he wished to, but the truth was that he *had* no wish to. He thought about what he had just done. He thought about the lies that he had just told.

He had just betrayed the Hive.

Before, he had just been an infected thing to be cured. If he had come clean to Purest Lux about what he was, then he might have been taken and changed back to what he was. Now that he had lied about it, there was no hope for any of that. All of this would result in his destruction now.

He had become a rebel against his own kind.

He should have felt guilt about that. He should have felt shame that he was no longer part of the great construction of the Hive. Instead, the only things he felt shame and guilt about were the things that the Hive had done. He was scared about what might happen to him, yes, but he was more frightened by the thought of what the Hive was doing to the universe.

He had become a rebel in his mind, in his emotions, in his speech. Now, he suspected, it was time for him to become one in his actions too.

CHAPTER TWELVE

"This is fun!" Luna yelled as she clung to the side of the school bus's front seat, bracing for the impact as its modified snowplow shoved another cluster of cars out of the way. She reached out with her free hand, catching hold of Bobby's collar so the sheepdog wouldn't tumble back along the length of the aisle.

"Maybe for you," their driver, a fat biker who incongruously wore a bandana featuring teddy bears, muttered.

"Ignore Trey," Cub said, beside Luna. "The bus was a great idea. Even if I do say so myself."

Luna turned to him. "Oh no, you are *not* claiming the bus was your idea."

"I saw it," Cub said.

"I saw it too," Luna insisted, and then caught Cub's grin. "You—"

What she might have said next was cut off by the next impact, which sent Bobby sliding down the middle of the bus despite Luna's attempts to hold on. The dog didn't seem to mind, treating it almost like a game and running back up to sit beside Luna, tail wagging.

"How far is it to LA?" Luna called over to Trey.

"You asking me if we're nearly there yet?" the driver grumbled.

"Trey," Cub said, with a warning note.

"Maybe half an hour, an hour?" Trey said.

"Depending on... well, I *guess* you could call it traffic?" Luna asked. "Can't we go any faster?"

She was only too aware of how little time they had. Although she was having fun smashing into things, every moment that passed was one step closer to the point where the aliens would take them over again, another moment in which the remaining aliens could ravage the world.

Trey shot her a look. "You want to try driving?"

Luna jumped up at once. "Can I?"

"It's probably best if Trey keeps driving," Cub suggested. "Given that he actually has a driver's license. He used to actually drive a bus before he joined the club, too."

That, Luna thought, explained a lot.

"If it's going to be that long before we hit LA," she said, "I'm going to check on Ignatius."

She glanced back to where the chemist was sitting on the back seat of the bus, which was empty except for him at the moment. It seemed that the members of the Dustsides gang weren't happy about spending too much time around him. He had gear spread out there, clinging onto it every time they hit a car, working with it in the spaces between.

"I'll shout to you once we get closer," Cub said. "Maybe while you're back there, work out what he's doing."

"I'll ask," Luna said, and made her way back through the bus with Bobby following. She went to sit on the back seat just as the bus hit something else, and Luna barely managed to put out a hand in time to catch a vial as it fell.

"Maybe this isn't the best time to be working on anything?" she suggested to Ignatius.

The chemist shrugged. "I have to do something, and it's not as if the bikers are going to talk to me."

"They have a pretty good reason, given what you used to do," Luna pointed out.

"Used to," Ignatius said. "It wasn't as though I had a lot of choice once I was in, and I… I'm trying to make up for it."

Luna thought that he probably meant it, but she wondered what it would take to make up for all the lives he'd probably helped to ruin. How many people would he have to save? How much good would he have to do to balance out the bad?

"What's so important that you're working on it on the back seat of the bus?" Luna asked. "Are you trying to improve the vaccine?"

Ignatius shook his head. "I'd need a proper lab to even start to work on that. I'm trying to work on an idea for what to do when the next person turns back."

When, not if, Luna noticed. It was hard to avoid the obvious question: who would it be, and when? Would it be her? Would it be Cub? That was the other thing that kept Ignatius separate from the group: he didn't have the lingering threat of transformation hanging over him.

"What *can* we do?" Luna asked. "When you're controlled, you don't feel pain, or tiredness, or anything. It means that you're faster and stronger than any normal person, and you don't stop until you've done what the aliens tell you to do."

"But they're not superhuman," Ignatius said.

"Are you sure? Because I'm pretty sure that I'm not as strong now as I was when I was controlled."

"From what you and the others have said, that's just because the aliens block a lot of the limits that the brain imposes on the body for its own safety. They don't actually make you stronger; they just let you use all of your strength."

"Like a grandmother pushing a car off of a kid," Luna said.

"Exactly. The body still responds. So what I'm working on is a sedative that will be strong enough to stun the body completely, so that we don't have to kill someone who turns."

"So you're just using a *lot* of sedative?" Luna asked. It seemed easy enough. You just took a lot of... well, of the kinds of things Ignatius used to make, and you pumped them into the transformed people.

"It's not that easy," Ignatius said. "The hard part with an anesthetic is never putting someone to sleep; it's doing it without shutting down the heart or the lungs. On someone whose body might not react in quite the same way... it's hard."

"It still sounds better than the alternative," Luna said. She reached out to put a hand over his. "And it's good that you're trying."

She went back up through the bus, watching as much of the landscape as was visible through the armor plates that they'd put in place. She hadn't thought that she would be heading back toward LA so soon. She'd *hoped* that she would be going home by now, after the virus had dealt with the aliens. She'd hoped that she would be driving back to see her parents, and that Kevin would be coming with her, and... and that everything would just be okay.

Luna picked one of the seats at the side, curling up in it with Bobby, not wanting Cub to see any of the tears that threatened to fall at those thoughts. It put her at the heart of the bikers, but Luna didn't mind that. For the most part, they seemed like good people, tough but actually pretty good now that she'd gotten to know them, as close with one another as Luna had been with...

Thoughts of Kevin and Chloe just made it worse.

"Ew!" Luna said as Bobby licked her face. "Yes, I know *you're* still here."

She hugged him tight, watching the landscape pass in desert shades and thinking about what it would be like if... *when* they finally managed to get rid of the aliens from Earth. There would still be so much to do, so many things to put right, but Luna wanted to believe that it would be better. It was a nice dream, at least.

She started to drift off, and then it *was* a dream, of going back to her house with Bobby, and her parents being there, and a boy who might have been Kevin or might have been Cub, because it seemed to shift every time she looked at him. Then, weirdly, the ground started to shake, and…

"Luna," Cub said, gently shaking her shoulder.

"Wha…" Luna managed sleepily. She hadn't realized quite how tired she was, but if she'd been sleepy enough to sleep through the bumps and crashes of the bus, she must have been pretty tired.

"We're getting close to LA," Cub said. "We need you to guide us to where the Survivors have made their camp."

"Okay," Luna said, getting up and dislodging Bobby, who had stayed beside her all this time. "Good dog."

She went down to the front of the bus, trying to get a sense of where they were.

"That way, I think," she said to Trey, who grunted a response.

They kept going, and Luna pointed the way to the driver, who didn't say much in response as he drove them up into the hills, to the spot Luna remembered from the last time she had been there. They wound their way around bends and on to the spot where fallen rocks marked the entrance to the canyon where the Survivors had their home.

"I should go first," Luna said, looking up to where the lookouts would be watching, waiting for them. "They know who I am."

"I'll go with you," Cub said.

"Huh," Trey agreed.

They got out of the bus, with Luna, Cub, and Bobby in the lead, Ignatius sticking fairly close by as if afraid of what might happen if he were left with the others, and the rest of the bikers following on behind. Trey was at the back, moving slowly.

Armed figures came down to meet them, Leon and Barnaby at their head. The Survivors' leader and the kid who had been clever enough to be accepted at college far too young looked over at Luna in surprise.

Luna was busy looking at the guns.

"Why have you brought guns out, guys?" she asked. "You can see it's me."

"And we *trust* you, Luna," Leon said. "But I don't know any of the rest of them, and plenty of them are adults, and the last I heard you were heading for the middle of Sedona with a way to stop the aliens."

"Did you do it?" Barnaby asked. "The world ship is gone. Is that because you and the others defeated them?"

Luna could hear the hope there, and she hated being the one who had to puncture that hope. As far as the Survivors knew, she,

Kevin, and Chloe might have succeeded and it was only a matter of time before their efforts filtered down into the rest of the aliens.

Better to do it quick, like ripping off a Band-Aid. Of course, ripping off Band-Aids still *hurt*.

"It didn't work," she said, trying to avoid looking too closely at their expressions. She didn't need to see their disappointment, because she could feel her own. "Chloe and Kevin sent up the vial, but *they* sent it back like it was nothing, like it was a joke, and then they took them."

"But not you?" Leon said. "I mean, you weren't with them?"

This, Luna suspected, was going to be the part that was hardest to explain. How was she supposed to tell them that she had become one of the controlled, and that she would be again? How was she supposed to get across the terror of that which filled her, and the hope that they might be able to—

A groan behind Luna cut her short. She spun to find Trey lurching forward, his movements angular and not at all human.

"No, not now," Luna said. "Not another one."

Trey surged forward, his arms extended to latch onto Ignatius's throat, squeezing. The members of the Survivors with guns lifted them again, aiming toward the struggling pair.

"No, don't!" Luna yelled. "Ignatius has a vaccine against being changed!"

That was enough to make them pause at least, and in that pause, Luna ran forward, hoping that there might be something that she could do to help. She kicked at Trey, hoping to distract him by drawing his attention to her, but it didn't seem to make any difference. She tried to pry his hands away from Ignatius's throat, but his fingers felt like steel. Luna could see Cub moving in close, a long knife in his hand, and she tried to think of something, anything, that would keep him from having to kill another member of his gang.

She saw that Ignatius was scrabbling at his pockets, trying to get to something. The chemist couldn't reach whatever it was, his struggles getting weaker with every passing moment. Luna risked reaching into his pocket and felt her hand close around something cold and hard.

She came out with a syringe, and knew what it had to be. Without hesitating, she plunged it into Trey, pressing down the plunger and hoping that it would do everything that Ignatius thought.

For a moment or two, nothing happened, and now Luna could see Ignatius starting to go limp in Trey's grip. When she tried pulling at his grip again, though, Luna found that grip coming loose. Trey turned toward her, took a step... and staggered. He kept coming forward, half upright, half crouched, until Luna did what seemed like the obvious thing and pushed him very gently.

Trey fell over and lay on his back, staring up white-eyed at the sky.

"It works!" Ignatius coughed, spluttering as he tried to get more breath inside him to celebrate. "My incapacitating injection works!"

"You're welcome," Luna said.

"What?" Ignatius asked, then frowned. "Oh, yes, of course, thank you. But without my injection..."

"You know," Luna said, "I'm starting to get why the others don't like you much."

Ignatius looked crestfallen. Cub, meanwhile, stared down at Trey's fallen form.

"What do we do with him?" he asked. "Do we... finish it?"

Luna could see he didn't want to, but she could also guess what he was thinking: that it was his job as the leader, and that there weren't many alternatives. Luna could think of at least one though.

"Have a couple of people take him away blindfolded," Luna said. "He's no danger like this, and if he can't see to find the way back, we're safe."

"*Are* you safe?" Leon asked, coming up to join them. "What just happened?"

"Trey just turned back," Cub answered.

"What do you mean 'turned back'?"

Luna knew that she needed to talk quickly. "Ignatius has a way to change people who are controlled back into humans. It also works as a vaccine for those who haven't ever been controlled. The trouble is, for the people who were controlled, it's only temporary."

Leon looked at her, then at Trey. "And how many of you..."

"All of us," Luna said. She sighed. "It's why I wasn't with Kevin and Chloe. It's why I'm not on that world ship of theirs. They changed me, and Ignatius turned me back."

"So at any moment you could turn into one of those things?" Leon said. He shook his head. "You shouldn't have come here, Luna. I have to think about my people. I can't let you in."

"Ignatius can make your people *immune*," Luna said. She got that Leon was all about protecting the people who looked up to him, but she wasn't about to let him turn them away now. They needed all the help they could get. "And I know you've heard rumors of a cure elsewhere. I thought between that and how clever Barnaby is, maybe we'd be able to find a way to make the cure permanent."

"And if you change into one of them?" Leon asked.

"Then you've already seen that there's a way to stop me," Luna said. She decided that it was a good moment to play her other card. "And who knows? Maybe we can work out why the virus that Barnaby assured us would work didn't."

"That's not fair," Leon said. "It's not his fault. He's clever, but he's just one kid."

"With us, and with Ignatius, you have a lot more than one kid," Luna said. "This is your best chance, Leon. *All* of our best chances."

Leon paused, looking around as if trying to gauge what kind of damage it would do if it went wrong. Luna already knew the answer to that: it could kill all of them.

Eventually though, Leon nodded.

"All right. But you get *that* out of here." He pointed to Trey. "And if any of you start to change and there isn't some special sedative around..."

"I know," Luna said. "You kill us."

CHAPTER THIRTEEN

Kevin considered the world that hung below them with the cool detachment of any member of the Hive. From where he stood, the screens let him see the settlements below, and the flares of movement down there. Once, the sight of it would have filled him with awe, or hope, or wonder. Now, it was merely a problem to be considered.

Once, the results of solving that problem might have made him feel guilty. Now, he just looked for ways to solve it faster.

"Will they try to strike at us?" Kevin asked Purest Lux.

The alien considered it for a few moments. "It is possible. They are unlikely to succeed."

Ships flew up from the surface, a cloud of them that seemed like a swarm of hornets closing in on the world ship. Like that, there seemed to be so many of them, yet as the Hive unleashed its own ships, it was clear that there weren't anywhere near enough. They attacked anyway, throwing themselves at the Hive, bursts of energy coming from their ships to smash into some of the Hive's ships. Kevin saw one and then another of the Hive's vessels burst apart like dandelions blown on by an angry storm.

There were more, though. The Hive could always build more. The Hive's vessels struck back, their attacks ripping into the ships that came at them, sending some to spin away, others to flare up in bursts of light that consumed them.

"Why do they keep attacking when they know they can't win?" Kevin asked Purest Lux, not understanding.

"Why do you think, Kevin?" Purest Lux asked. "Think back to your life before you joined us. Think about the ways people act when they have the curse of emotions."

Kevin tried to think. It was surprisingly difficult to do; the time before he had become a part of the Hive seemed like another life entirely. He'd had emotions then, but it still took an effort for him to understand them now, and what they might mean. It felt as though they were there behind a kind of curtain imposed by his membership of the Hive. He was grateful for it. It meant that he no longer had the weakness of emotions.

"Perhaps they want to feel like they tried everything," Kevin suggested. "Perhaps they feel as though fighting is better than just giving in." Another possibility occurred to him. "Perhaps they're buying time for people to escape."

"A good thought," Purest Lux said. "We will watch for ships seeking to flee under cover of the battle, and destroy them."

Kevin watched with the Purest, but surprisingly few ships seemed to come up from the surface in this phase of the attack.

"Why aren't more running?" Kevin asked. It made no sense to him. Why would they stay there when they were about to die?

"Perhaps they think they can fight us off," Purest Lux suggested. "They believe themselves to be entirely safe behind their shields. They would even be correct, if it were not for you. Study them, Kevin. Learn the things that the Hive has gathered, so that you will know the enemy we are about to destroy."

Kevin delved into the collective knowledge of the Hive, seeking information on the world that their ship now orbited. The information flowed into him, not like something he was learning for the first time, but more like something he'd always known and was only now remembering.

The creatures on the world below were called Ilari. They were slightly smaller than humans, with blue-gray skin and nodules that dotted them at spaced intervals, links to twinned AIs that, bizarrely, didn't seem to join into the kind of collective mind that the Hive possessed. Kevin couldn't understand that. Here was a species with the resources to create its own kind of Hive, and yet it chose not to.

Even so, they were not to be underestimated. They were clever, resourceful, inventive... and possessed of some of the most advanced technology the Hive had seen. The shield they had put around the world below was just one example.

And, strangely, the Hive was... concerned about them. Not scared, because fear was as alien to it as any other emotion, but aware of the threat that such advanced foes could pose to even their continued existence.

Their conventional weapons were dangerous enough: they had skills in the manipulation of energy that gave them powerful shields and beam weapons now that they had realized the danger that being without defenses presented.

The bigger danger, though, came from the understanding they had of the Hive. The same AIs that didn't connect to one another in their society could potentially be used to disrupt the Hive's connection. With enough knowledge, they might be able to disrupt the nanobots at the heart of the Hive's controlling vapor. They could disrupt all that the Hive was, potentially threatening its very existence.

Kevin considered the knowledge that he had just gained. It was the kind of knowledge that had the potential to destroy the Hive. With it, a foe with the right materials would be able to tune a signal that would be a weapon, not just against individual ships, but against all of them. It required a substance called miridium that Kevin had never heard of, but that the Hive's records suggested could be found on Earth.

It explained why the Hive had been so eager to take Earth, where the minerals that such a signal could be focused through could be found, and why these foes were so high on their list of enemies to destroy.

"And I will destroy them," Kevin said.

"*We* will destroy them," Purest Lux corrected him. "You will provide the way, though, Kevin. Do you feel any remorse at that?"

For a moment, Kevin wondered if Purest Lux might be making some kind of joke, but he suspected that wasn't something that the Purest did. No, he realized, it was a test to make sure that he remained as he should be: connected to the heart of the Hive, without the weaknesses that came from being beyond it.

"I feel only the honor of being chosen, Purest Lux," Kevin said. "And I am grateful to the Hive for all that it has done for me."

The Hive had saved him. His connection to it had put him beyond the threat posed by his former illness, and beyond so many other human concerns. He would not age as humans aged, would not be touched by disease or weakness. He would never achieve the perfection that the Purest had, but in time, Kevin had no doubt that they would change him to make him better and stronger.

"I will do all that I can for the good of the Hive."

"Yes," Purest Lux assured him, "you will. We will begin with communications. Convince them, Kevin. Persuade them to open the way."

Kevin nodded, and stood in a clear section of the floor. A light shone down on him, and an image shimmered in the air, a holographic representation serving as a kind of screen. On it, Kevin saw blue-skinned figures, young and old, tall and short, looking as varied as any crowd on Earth might have done. In their way, they looked far *more* varied than the inhabitants of the Hive. Oh, that had dozens of different species and variations within it, but they were not the Purest, and the Purest had a strange kind of similarity to one another, barely seeming to vary.

One of the Ilari, an older-looking female, stood toward the front. She spoke before Kevin could.

"I am General s'Lara," she said, and as with the Hive, Kevin's mind translated the words automatically. "Who are you, and why are you aboard one of the Hive's world ships?"

Kevin thought quickly, trying to come up with a lie that would convince the creatures below. He realized that being the emotionless drone of the Hive wouldn't work. He needed to at least pretend to be who he had been.

"My name's Kevin McKenzie," he said. "You sent me messages. You warned my world. I was the one who heard."

"You? Are you a leader amongst your people?"

Kevin shook his head. "I'm just a kid. I'm just..." He tried to think quickly. "I'm no one really."

"Then what are you doing on the Hive's ship?" the general asked.

"Your message helped," Kevin said. "It gave us the advice we needed. My friends and I managed to find a virus buried deep in a tar pit. We raced all the way to Sedona to use it on them. We had to fight our way through the people that they controlled. We did it though. We infected them with the virus, and... it worked."

"It worked?" General s'Lara said.

"We beat them," Kevin said. "We took their world ship, we broke some of them free of their Hive."

"Then why are you here?" General s'Lara demanded. "Why are you attacking us?"

"*You* attacked *us*," Kevin said, grateful for that detail. "I'm sorry. We overreacted. We'll pull our people back."

He looked over to Purest Lux, who nodded. On the screens around Kevin, he saw the attack ships pulling back to surround the world ship.

"You still haven't said why you're here," the general said.

"We need your help," Kevin said. "We've managed to take down this world ship, but we barely managed to get it here. We don't really know what we're doing. Even the former members of the Hive have lost so much knowledge. If we're going to take on the rest, then we all need to work together."

It was the best lie he could think of, the kind of impassioned plea that he might have made if he had really been disconnected from the Hive. In a way, it was like living out some alternative life, where his pitiful efforts to destroy the Hive with Chloe and Luna had succeeded.

Kevin could see other members of the Ilari paying attention now, looking as if they weren't sure whether to dare to believe what he was saying or not.

"What do you need from us?" General s'Lara asked.

"We've come a long way, and some of our people need your help," Kevin said. "Can we come down to the surface? Will you lower your shields for us?"

General s'Lara stared at him, then shook her head. "We can bring help and supplies up to you if you need them. For the moment, I'm not sure that it would be a good idea for us to lower the shields."

"Please," Kevin said. "You have to, we need to be able to come down to the surface."

He saw the general's expression harden, then shift to something approaching pity.

"Our warning didn't come in time, did it?" she asked.

Kevin might have kept trying, but Purest Lux stepped up next to him then, putting a hand on his shoulder to stop him.

"Tell them the truth," the Purest said. "Tell them that nothing can stop the Hive, and that they have a choice now. They can submit and be transformed, or they can be destroyed. Tell them."

Kevin relayed the words, his mind translating them automatically for him.

"I'm sorry," General s'Lara said. "We thought that we could save people before they suffered the way we did. Tell your Hive friends that they will not get through our shields, and that our energy weapons are online. We might not be able to kill all of their kind, but we have enough power to destroy a great many of them before their end, including their precious Purest."

Kevin didn't relay the message, because he knew what the Hive's answer would be. "You should surrender," he said. "Being a part of the Hive is wonderful. Why wouldn't you want it? Why would you want to be destroyed when you could be a fragment of something *amazing*?"

"Because we aren't just fragments," General s'Lara said. "If you attack us, we will fight."

"You'll lose," Kevin promised.

The connection cut. Kevin turned to Purest Lux.

"Forgive me, Purest, I have failed the Hive."

"Not yet," Purest Lux replied. "It was always unlikely that a species that has fallen to us on other worlds would let us in on this one. You still have a role to play in bringing down their shields."

"Yes, Purest Lux."

Kevin saw ships start to detach from the world ship: small, rapid hunter craft that were like the scavenger ships that had gone to the surface of his world, only better armed; and much larger city ships, which floated like great manta rays down toward the atmosphere of the world.

The first of the hunter craft slammed into the Ilarians' shield bursting apart on impact in a ripple of force that lit it up and showed the shimmering blue of its outline. Kevin stared at it, trying to understand it.

An energy beam spiked up from the surface, bright and pure, and for an instant, there was a hole in the shields for it to punch through. It slammed into the side of one of the city ships, tearing off a chunk and sending it listing to one side.

"Do you see the way the shield parts for their weapon?" Purest Lux asked, apparently ignoring the way so many of their forces had been damaged in the first few moments of conflict.

"Purest Lux," Kevin said, "they have damaged a city ship. Isn't that a bad thing?"

"There are no Purest aboard," Purest Lux said, by way of an answer, as another blast of energy came up from the surface, lancing into space as it missed its target. "Focus, Kevin."

"Yes, Purest Lux. How does the shield part?"

"There is a signal," Purest Lux said. "These creatures trust their machines to time everything, and the machines focus on a signal. Our scanners can pick up every signal from the surface, and once they do…"

"I should be able to understand it," Kevin said.

"You *will* understand it," Purest Lux insisted. "You will pick out the correct signal and work out what to send. This is why we took you into the Hive. The signal will be sent through here for you."

Kevin stood there waiting, hoping that he would be able to do all that Purest Lux asked of him. The Hive was depending on him, and he would not let it down. He listened while the world ship's systems sent up every signal they could find. Kevin listened to them all, straining his ears for every hint of something that might be relevant. He heard encrypted military communications, heartfelt messages from families frightened for one another, pleas for help, and…

There.

He latched onto the signal while another energy blast came, this one making the world ship shake as it hit. His brain worked feverishly to translate it, and numbers spilled from his mouth almost in a dream. He could feel the Hive taking them and sending them out in their own signal, using them to target the shield.

Below, the hunter ships continued to plunge toward the shield, but now they didn't break against it. Now, they plunged lower, and lower still. Kevin saw the shield ripple and die, fading to nothingness in the face of the Hive's fleet.

"I've done it," he said. "The shield is down."

"Very good, Kevin," Purest Lux said. "Now, let us show them what a true weapon can do. Get ready to destroy this world."

CHAPTER FOURTEEN

Around her, Luna heard the beating of hammers and the quiet hiss of welding torches as the Survivors and the bikers worked together to create everything they might need in the face of the alien threat.

That, it turned out, was a lot of stuff.

Leon and Cub had set up a kind of production lines for weapons, with anything that could hold an edge or shoot an improvised arrow pressed into service. Luna wasn't sure if she liked that. She wanted the aliens gone, but killing people who were just under their control wouldn't do any good.

"We could end up killing a lot of innocent people," Luna said to Bobby, who wandered along at her side as they made their way through the Survivors' cave complex. She suspected that the others wouldn't listen to her if she said it to them, though.

Maybe she was just very aware that soon, she might be one of those people again. Luna found herself watching every movement she made, and every thought she had, trying to make sure that they were her own, not something else's. She could feel herself becoming more worried with every hour that passed, every hint of tiredness feeling as though it might turn into losing herself completely.

She tried to think about the signs that there had been from Bear and then from Trey: they'd seemed sleepier, hadn't said as much, hadn't really responded to questions with more than a grunt or two. They'd seemed to shuffle about, not really in control of themselves, or perhaps just *losing* control of themselves.

"Will I know when it happens?" Luna asked herself. Last time she had. She'd known that she was slipping away, and had even been able to fight it, if only for a second or two. Maybe this time would be the same. Maybe she would be able to feel it coming and get to the antidote in time.

"Assuming we *have* an antidote by then," Luna said to Bobby. He pushed against her reassuringly.

She went over to the space where Ignatius and Barnaby were working, neither one quite anyone's idea of a normal scientist, yet the two together looking as though they were making good progress. Barnaby was looking through a microscope at something, while Ignatius seemed to be giving his vaccine to a line of different members of the Survivors.

"This should protect you against all chance of being converted," he said as he passed a vial of it to a man who didn't look certain about it at all. "Drink it all."

Ignatius looked over at Luna.

"Ah, there you are. I was getting worried. It's just about time for your next boost of the vaccine."

"Is it helping?" Luna asked. "Is it slowing any of it down?"

"I believe so," Ignatius said. "It's hard to say for sure, and I suspect some of it may just be that some people are more susceptible to relapsing than others. Still…"

He held up another vial of the substance, and Luna took it with a grimace. It tasted awful as she drank it. Still, it left her feeling a little more certain that she was in control of herself, a little more able to focus. That was the important thing.

"We'll need to make more soon," Ignatius said. "I have administered it to most of the Survivors, but you and the bikers still need more, and we should have some ready to use on more of the controlled."

"And you can just make more?" Luna asked.

"It isn't that hard now that I know the correct formula for it, and I think they have everything I'll need here. You can help me if you like."

Luna was going to say no, but she realized that it would sound pretty ungrateful, relying on a substance to survive that she wasn't prepared to help cook up. Besides, Ignatius had been pretty helpful so far. It also seemed like a good idea to know how to make the thing that could potentially save her life.

"*Can* I help?" Luna asked.

"So long as you watch carefully and do what I say," Ignatius replied.

Luna started to help, fetching ingredients from the Survivors' limited stores and helping to mix them, boil them, and separate them. It reminded her a little of being in science lab at school, only with a partner who was the only one who knew how the experiment they were doing worked. Bobby sat at the side the whole time, watching on as if he might be able to learn how to do it.

"Do you have a centrifuge?" Ignatius asked Barnaby, who looked up from his microscope and nodded.

"We managed to take a bunch of lab equipment from one of the colleges. I figured it might come in useful."

Ignatius showed Luna how to use it to separate samples, and got to work on what looked like another batch of the sedative he'd used on Trey.

"Is that for the next person who turns?" Luna asked.

"Maybe," Ignatius said. "Barnaby pointed out that if we made some dart guns, we might have a way to bring down the controlled from a distance. For a kid, he's pretty smart."

Luna wasn't sure if he meant that as a compliment or a reminder of how young Barnaby still was.

"Leon has a couple of the others building dart guns out of whatever we can scavenge," Barnaby said. He still didn't look up from his microscope.

"What's so interesting there?" Luna asked, going over to him with Bobby. "You've been looking at the same thing since I got here."

"It's a sample of Cub's blood," Barnaby said. He looked up, looking thoughtful. "Actually, yes... Luna, can I take a sample of your blood too?"

"I... guess so," Luna said. Barnaby came up with a needle that seemed far too big. "Um... what exactly do you need this for?"

"To compare to Cub's blood, so I can see if I'm right about what I'm thinking," he explained.

Luna managed to hold still while Barnaby took a sample of her blood, taking a drop of it and placing it on a slide to examine.

"You needed a needle that size for one drop?" Luna said.

"Well, it means that I have a blood sample to do more work with," Barnaby said, then shrugged. "Why? Afraid of needles?"

"I'm not afraid of anything," Luna said, running her hand through Bobby's hair. That wasn't true. She was afraid of all kinds of things. It was just that a lot of the big things, like losing everyone she cared about, or something really bad happening to everything around her, had already kind of... happened. Compared to that, the small things didn't seem so important.

Barnaby smiled and then moved over to the microscope, staring down it. "Interesting, the resurgence isn't quite as quick in this sample. Maybe there's something about you that puts you closer to the right chemical composition."

"What are you talking about, Barnaby?" Luna asked.

"I think I know why the vaccine hasn't worked completely to free people from being controlled by the aliens," he said. "Looking at the samples, their 'vapor' is actually a cloud of tiny robots, so small they can't be seen."

"Nanobots," Ignatius said, looking up from the formula he was concocting with an interested expression.

"I had thought it would be a disease, but this makes more sense, because it tells us some of why the aliens are able to control people."

"Does it tell us how to get rid of them?" Luna asked, her hand tightening for a moment in Bobby's fur.

"From our bodies or from the world?" Barnaby asked, and then shook his head. "I don't think it's that simple."

"Knowing the problem doesn't give you an answer," Ignatius agreed. "But you said that looking at the sample told you why the vaccine wasn't working perfectly on people who were already infected with them."

Barnaby nodded at that.

"When you look closely at the blood samples from Cub and Luna, they have some of the nanobots, and the vaccine compound locks together with them, making them harmless. They're not a perfect fit though."

"Because they weren't designed for this," Luna guessed. "It's a side effect, not something Ignatius's vapor was originally designed to do."

She saw Ignatius nod. "That makes sense."

"Does that mean that we can improve it?" Luna asked, not daring to hope. "Could we make it a better fit to get rid of them altogether?"

She saw Barnaby take a breath and knew that the answer wasn't going to be a simple yes.

"In theory, we could," Barnaby said. "In theory, it might even be possible to communicate with the nanites using the right kind of signal and disrupt them once they're linked with. Both options seem to require the same kind of material."

"What material?" Luna asked. She glanced down at Bobby, as much for reassurance as anything. The dog sat there wagging his tail.

"That's the problem," Barnaby said. "I don't know."

Luna looked across to Ignatius. "What about you? Didn't you *design* chemical compounds?"

The chemist shrugged. "I did, and given enough time, I *might* be able to improve the fit with the nanobots, but we'd be talking months of work, even if I succeeded."

Months, not days. Luna understood what he was saying: that by the time he came up with any kind of answer, it would be too late for Luna and the other bikers, maybe too late for what was left of Earth.

"There has to be *something*," Luna insisted.

Ignatius seemed unconvinced by that. "Life doesn't work like that. No one said it was fair. No one said that doing the right thing meant that you got to win."

"So why are *you* trying to do the right thing?" Luna demanded. "If you really believe that, why did you come and try to save people with that vapor gun you made? Why take the risk?"

Ignatius was quiet for a long time.

"There are materials labs in UCLA," he said. "Some of them test samples from around the world, others create new substances. Our best hope of finding something in time would be to look for something that already exists."

He still said it like he didn't believe that there was any real hope, but just the fact that he was willing to make that much effort made Luna think a little better of him. She looked over to Barnaby.

"What do you think?" she asked. "Would we be able to identify what we needed if we found it?"

"Maybe," Barnaby said. "We have the blood samples, so if we find anything close, we can try it on them."

"So all we need to do is go there, look for what we need, and maybe we can stop me from turning back into one of... *them*?"

Hope built up inside Luna, just a small spark, but she wanted it to be true.

"I don't think it will be that simple," Barnaby said. "You've seen what it can be like in the city."

Luna had seen it. She'd seen the blockades and the controlled. She guessed that Leon wouldn't like the idea of putting his people at risk just on the hope of finding something.

"We'll do it, though, won't we?" she asked. She was worried by the thought that they might not, and that she would be left sitting there, waiting to change back into one of the controlled. "We have to."

"I think it's our best chance," Barnaby said. "We have the vaccine, but so many people are already controlled. It won't help them."

"It won't help me," Luna said.

"No," Barnaby agreed. "We need to do it. We just need to persuade Leon."

"Cub and the others will want to go," Luna said. "But for this... I think we'll need help."

93

Barnaby nodded his agreement. "I'll talk to Leon, and we have weapons that can help now."

Luna thought about the dart guns and the vapor gun Ignatius had built.

"We still need more," she said.

"We have some real guns, and some knives and swords," Barnaby said. "They can stop the controlled."

"Kill them?" Luna said. "These are people. They can't feel anything, but they're still in there. We have to be able to get them back."

It seemed as though there were two choices right then; two ways the world might turn out. They had the vaccine now, so the people who hadn't already been controlled could stay that way forever. The only question was what happened with the controlled.

The best option, the one Luna was really hoping for, was that they would find a way to free the controlled permanently, taking away the aliens' power over the world and releasing everyone to fight back. If they managed that, then there might be enough of them to win. There *had* to be a reason the aliens had used this way of invading, rather than just attacking outright. Maybe they feared that humanity might have some way to damage them?

The other option was a war between the people who were controlled and the ones who weren't. It would be a war that the aliens won whatever happened, because there would be so few humans left to fight them. Worse, it would be a war where Luna, Cub, and the others would be on the wrong side in just a few days. It couldn't happen. They had to—

Bells and sirens sounded around the caves that housed the Survivors. Luna ran out, Bobby loping along beside her, to find Leon out in the canyon that protected them, giving orders.

"Hannah, Eddie, on the far side! You three, get into the rocks there! I want everyone who can hold a weapon out here now!"

"What's happening?" Luna asked, stepping into Leon's path. "Leon, what's going on?"

"The aliens are attacking," Leon said.

"How many?" Luna asked. Just the look on Leon's face gave her a bad feeling about this.

"Come look," Leon said.

He led the way up through some of the rocks to one of the lookout points. From there, Luna could see the mass of figures below, moving together in synchronization, heading for the hideout. Trey was in amongst them, and Luna knew then that they'd made a mistake letting the biker go. He'd been able to show the aliens where they were, and after that, it had only been a matter of time.

It seemed that they would get a chance to test out their new weaponry sooner than Luna had expected. The controlled were coming for them, and if the Survivors didn't stop them, it didn't matter if they'd been vaccinated. The aliens would simply kill every single person there.

CHAPTER FIFTEEN

Kevin watched the battle for the planet below unfold with the same interest he might have had in a new video game. It seemed almost the same, with bright flashes of light as blasts of energy struck, and the rapid dance of spacecraft in deadly combat. He tried to consider what he felt about the fact that there were people killing and dying out there in the blackness around the planet, but it felt like a foolish question. Why should he feel anything, when he was one of the Hive?

He considered the Ilarian fighting ships, which moved and turned with the speed of a school of silver fish, weapons picking Hive craft out of space with the deadliness of razors. Each took out more than its share of Hive fighter craft as they moved closer to the world, bursting five or six at a time into fields of debris that seemed to create a dust storm in a place without air to carry it. They darted in and away, harrying the Hive's ships, but not all of them made it. With each pass, fewer and fewer of the silver ships made it.

"Why are they standing and fighting?" Kevin asked. "They could run."

"You already know the answer to that," Purest Lux pointed out.

Kevin blinked. Of course he did. He'd been the one to tell Purest Lux that they were sacrificing their lives to try to save others of their kind. It seemed hard to remember why though, and harder still to believe that any creature could really think and feel like that. The good of the Hive was one thing, but trying to save weak creatures that had no use?

"The way they're darting in and out is costing us ships," Purest Lux said.

"They're trying to draw our ships away," Kevin guessed. "They want to strike at the larger ships."

"That is part of it," Purest Lux agreed. "You seem to have a feel for this, Kevin. Perhaps we have a role for you in this assault. Come."

Purest Lux led the way to a chair, with the now familiar connections that would allow interface with the world ship's systems. It seemed so much less elegant than the pure, organic connection to the Hive that filled Kevin's mind.

As soon as Kevin sat, though, he had to admit that the connection was amazing. It was as though his mind could flit from ship to ship, seeing from the cameras and the sensors, giving orders to the systems, sitting in the pilot's seat in every sense except the physical.

The battle raged around him now, in missile streaks and energy bursts. Kevin sent a ship left, then right, into a roll that lined it up with one of the enemy ships. He fired, and the ship was already moving away, sweeping in an arc that was hard to match.

"They're not standing and fighting," Kevin said, knowing that Purest Lux would hear.

"Make them," Purest Lux said.

Kevin knew what he meant. Shifting his attention to the other ships, he picked out the spots where vessels were trying to leave the surface and break free. He sent the smaller vessels after them sharp and direct, not caring about the numbers that were destroyed on such an obvious course. There were pilot creatures in the vessels, but they would only be grateful to fall for the Hive.

The ships grew closer, and Kevin saw one of the fleeing vessels move into the crosshairs of one of the craft his consciousness flitted between. He watched it there, a fat and easy target, and considered that once, he would have thought that what he was about to do was evil beyond measuring. He couldn't think why now; it was for the good of the Hive, not against it.

Without hesitating, Kevin fired.

Energy lanced through the darkness of space, ripping through the hull of one of the fleeing ships. At first, nothing happened, because the Hive's hunter ship was small, and the escape craft was large enough to take a wound like that; a whale bitten only once by a shark.

Then, taking their cue from the first shot, a dozen others fired on the ship, shattering it into pieces that spread as they broke from the hull, the creatures within spinning into space. Perhaps some were protected by suits, but soon there would be nothing to rescue them. They would drift, and they would die.

It occurred to Kevin that he knew exactly what it felt like to know that you were going to die, but not to know how long it would be. Was that... empathy? No. He would have to feel something for that. This was just knowledge, memory... that was all it was.

At the back of his mind, Kevin could almost hear something shouting at him, yelling that this was wrong, that there was more than just the Hive. He turned to it, trying to understand the curiosity of it. He felt as though he almost had it...

The connection to the ship cut in a blaze of light as the defenders' ships swept in, destroying the Hive's first wave of fighters. They were fast, and it wasn't just how quickly they could cross the distance there, or turn. Each ship seemed to react with a speed that Kevin couldn't match, taking bewildering twists and turns that made it hard to even begin thinking about the move they were making before they were away into the next one.

"They're too fast," Kevin said, the strain of trying to keep up with them pushing at the edges of his brain, feeling as though it might sheer in half from the effort.

"It is not about being fast," Purest Lux said. "Find other ways. The AIs are their strength, but what is their weakness?"

"Emotions," Kevin said. "The computers... they want to keep their pilots alive, right?"

"Exactly," Purest Lux said.

The Hive showed him the foolishness of that. There were weaker creatures and stronger ones. The pilots of their craft were not of the Purest. They could be sacrificed. What other advantages did the Hive have? They were not singular. They could work as a whole.

Kevin reached out to the Hive's ships, spreading them out into a net to contain the faster ships of the enemy. He turned them in toward the center and started them forward, firing as they went.

They hit their own ships. Again and again, Kevin found the connection to ships cut. Again and again, he jumped to new ones, charging forward. Some of the silvery ships of the defenders charged back at him, but he didn't pull up, didn't stop. The computers there might have been able to pull out of the maneuver at the last possible millisecond, but what could they do against an enemy who truly wouldn't pull back, because the Hive's will meant everything?

As the defending fighters started to disperse or fall, Kevin turned his attention to the surface. The city ships were there, striking down with cascades of energy, viruses, and poisons that filled the air, yet great bursts of power came up from the surface too, and only the slowness with which they came stopped more of the city ships from being destroyed.

Some still were, and although nothing in the Hive could feel the pain of loss, Kevin knew that a city ship contained more creatures, and was harder to replace than any smaller ship. He saw the energy beams from the surface lance into them and through, leaving holes that could only be sealed by closing bulkheads and hoping to repair vital systems in time. He saw one of the great ships tear in half like a broken plate, another drop to the side and start to burn up as it hit the atmosphere at the wrong angle.

"We can't lose so many," Kevin said.

"We lose as many as we must," Purest Lux replied. "The destruction of this enemy is all that matters."

Even so, Kevin knew that he had to at least try to save the city ships. He took another of the Hive's fast hunter ships, flying it and a squadron of others down beneath the shell of the atmosphere, seeing the red sparks fly up as they pushed in at a steep angle. He knew where the last of the blasts had come from, and he flew for it, twisting and angling the fighter craft as smaller weapons shot his way. One ship went down, and he switched to another, then another.

The great gun came into view, looking more like one of the radio telescopes that SETI might have used than like a weapon. Even so, Kevin could see the power thrumming on its surface, could feel the shields around it, meant to protect it. His brain found the codes to bring them down in an instant, translating automatically.

He slammed the ship he was controlling into the cannon's side, the explosion ripping through it and spreading as the energy it had been building up rippled out, uncaged. He took a moment to look down on the beauty of it, spreading out like waves on a pond, but it was only a moment. He was already moving on to the next weapon, and the next.

How many ships did they lose in the attack? Kevin didn't even try to keep track of it, but he was sure that the Hive would have a record of it somewhere and he was just as sure that the number would stagger anyone who didn't understand the way the Hive worked. Losing so many to conquer a world like this didn't matter. All that mattered was that the enemy was defeated.

Except… in spite of all of it, the enemy *weren't* being defeated.

"So many of their defenses are down," Kevin said, pulling out of the connection to look at Purest Lux, "but they refuse to give up. They should submit to the inevitable. Their computers—"

"Their computers are as individual as they are," Purest Lux said. "They think in terms of a single, perfect partnership of creature and machine, creature and beloved others. They cannot understand what it is to be nothing, even when they are."

Kevin was about to say that he couldn't understand that, but he found himself thinking of Luna, and of Chloe. They were images from a past before the Hive that shouldn't have mattered, because any life without the Hive was incomplete, but he still thought of them. Luna was the kind of person who would fight even though the odds seemed hopeless. Chloe was so filled with emotion that it would fuel her through any battle.

"They will keep fighting," Kevin said, sounding surprised even to himself. "They will keep fighting right down to the last of them." He thought of the Hive, and how it worked. "It will make it difficult to strip this world of its resources before it is destroyed."

"With these enemies, it does not matter," Purest Lux said. "They came as close to destroying us as anyone has. They found the secret. Eliminating that is more important even than acquiring more resources for the Hive."

That was a huge statement, given that the world ships existed purely to gather resources for the Hive's home world. Even so, Kevin had seen the danger that might be posed by the ideas the Ilarians had dreamed up, and particularly by the substance that they could not find: miridium.

"The destruction will take time," Kevin said. "I am doing all I can, Purest Lux, but the battle is still difficult."

Every enemy ship was dangerous, every soldier seemed to have weapons that could harm them. Kevin might have found ways to force them to fight on the Hive's terms, but how many more surprises would their foes have for them?

"The battle does not matter, Kevin," Purest Lux said.

Kevin frowned at that. "It doesn't matter?"

"It is serving its purpose by keeping the enemy away from the world ship and letting us stay in position while power builds up." Purest Lux moved away from the seat. "Come with me, Kevin. See for yourself."

Purest Lux led the way to a viewing balcony on the side of the spire. There, the alien looked up, toward the glowing heart of the world ship. Kevin wasn't sure what he was supposed to be looking at.

"Look closer, Kevin," Purest Lux said. "Doesn't it look... different, to you?"

Kevin tried to think what it had looked like when he first arrived, but even then, it took him a moment to understand. When he and Chloe had first arrived on the world ship, its heart had glowed like a miniature sun, radiating its energy in every direction in a golden glow. Now, the glow seemed tighter, but also brighter, white hot and focused, pulling inward as if preparing for something. Kevin started as energy crackled from the tips of the golden spires, feeding into the heart like lightning somehow forking upward.

"Soon the energy will have built up enough," Purest Lux said. "And then it will be ready to unleash."

"Unleash how?" Kevin asked.

Purest Lux gestured, and Kevin looked over to the spot he indicated. There, Kevin saw a whole section of the world ship start to curl back on itself, opening like the iris on a camera. There must have been some kind of shield or something there to hold air inside the hollow core of the ship, because a hole the size of... well, so big that Kevin couldn't *think* of anything it might be the size of, started to open up into space.

Through it, like looking out through a single giant eye, Kevin could see the world below.

"It's a weapon," Kevin said. "The whole ship is a weapon."

"It is," Purest Lux said. "And soon, it will be ready to fire."

CHAPTER SIXTEEN

Luna stared at the advancing horde of controlled in horror. She hadn't seen this many in one place before, even when they'd been at the NASA institute, even when they'd been on the docks trying to get to LA. There were so many there now that it seemed like a sea of them, all moving in concert, sweeping toward the canyon where the Survivors made their home.

Luna saw the others there just staring at them as they came forward, and that was enough to snap her out of her own horror.

"Don't just stand there," she shouted. "We have to fight them!"

The shout was enough to remind the Survivors of what they were meant to be doing. The ones with guns opened fire, the crack of them deafening against the silence with which the controlled advanced. The ones with tools and knives, improvised swords and other close range weapons moved to block the entrance to the Survivors' camp.

Some of the controlled went down, brought down by the gunfire. The ones hit anywhere that wasn't vital kept going, but the ones hit in the head or shot through the heart toppled over, just as anyone else would have. Luna winced with each one who fell, knowing that it was a person, and that it could just as easily have been her.

That it might *still* be her, soon enough.

"Try to use the weapons we've been making!" she called out, even though she knew that against so many of the controlled, they would have to use every weapon they could find just to survive.

Even so, she saw some of the Survivors do it, picking up dart guns and nets, doing their best to incapacitate the controlled without killing the people who were still in there somewhere, buried deep. Luna picked up a dart gun too, along with a stock of the sedative darts that had brought down Trey the first time. She fired down into the mass of controlled and reloaded, fired and reloaded. Beside her, Bobby snarled, as if he might be able to scare them off from her. Ignatius passed her darts as she fired.

"There are too many of them to stay here," Leon said, and he sounded angry about it. Luna could guess why.

"We didn't know that coming here would lead the aliens to you," she said.

"The moment your bus driver turned, they knew," Leon said. He shook his head. "That doesn't matter now. We have to evacuate the people who are too weak to fight, but to do that..."

"We'll hold them," Luna promised, knowing what Leon was scared of: that the moment he wasn't here, the entranceway would fall. Luna fired down again, bringing down another of the controlled. There were more. She suspected that there would *always* be more.

She ran down to the entranceway below as the controlled surged against it. She couldn't help to push them back, because she didn't have enough size or weight for that, but she could help to build up the barricade there, grabbing anything that looked heavy enough to slow someone down and dragging it into place. It wasn't as easy as when she'd been controlled, and it hurt now, but Luna ignored the pain.

At the barricades she helped build, the Dustsides bikers and the Survivors fought, striking at the controlled with their improvised weapons, pushing them back and cutting them down even as they continued to push forward. Some shot at them with the dart guns, and so did Luna in the spaces between dragging in more materials to block the way.

One of the controlled broke through, running at her and grabbing her, faster than Luna could react. It breathed out a wash of vapor that enveloped her, seeming to fill the world, and for a moment, Luna felt herself remembering what it had been like the first time with the vapor running through her blood, taking her over. She remembered what it had been like to lose herself the first time, and fear flooded through her. Would it happen again now? Would she be nothing but one of the controlled again?

Bobby slammed into the side of the thing, knocking it away from Luna, and she lifted the dart gun, shooting it.

"Good boy," Luna said, ruffling Bobby's fur.

On the barriers, the other controlled were breathing out their vapor, trying to change the people fighting there. The bikers and the Survivors kept fighting though, unchanged. The bikers had already been infected and cured. The Survivors had Ignatius's vaccine running in their systems. It meant that they could keep going, keep fighting, keep bringing down the controlled who came at them.

The controlled seemed to realize that something was wrong, or if they didn't, the aliens controlling them did. They paused, as if thinking, or perhaps receiving new orders, and then they surged forward again, striking with renewed violence. They weren't trying to grab people and change them now; instead, they were striking out with hands and feet, trying to hurt; trying to kill.

Luna saw one of the bikers dragged down. She saw Cub lashing out left and right with a sharpened length of metal, forcing back the controlled. She saw Leon further back, guiding a line of small children who had no hope of being able to hold back the controlled, trying to get them out of the caves. Another of the controlled ran at Luna and Bobby snarled, biting at one who had been an old woman before the aliens changed her. Now she rushed forward with the deadly silence that all of them did. Luna shot her with the dart gun, watching her fall, then went to reload.

"I need more darts!" Luna called out, looking around for Ignatius.

She saw him further away, running as if his life depended on it. Luna could understand the fear, but she needed him, they *all* did, and anger rose in her at the thought that he was trying to abandon them.

"Bobby," she shouted, pointing. "Fetch!"

Maybe it was the fact that he was a sheepdog, or maybe he was as annoyed as she was that Ignatius was running away, but he raced off after Ignatius at the same time Luna did, pulling ahead of her and bowling the chemist over in a way that looked as much about exuberance as a meaningful attempt to stop him. Bobby sat in front of him, tongue lolling, just watching him while Luna caught up.

"Where do you think you're going?" Luna demanded as Ignatius stood, and it felt weird, talking to an adult like that, but right then she didn't care.

"We have to get out of here," Ignatius said. "They're starting to break through."

"We *all* need to get out of here," Luna said, "which means that we need to hold them back. We need your vapor guns, Ignatius."

"But—"

"You were willing to wade into a crowd of us to save me and the others," Luna said. "There's obviously a part of you that wants to do the right thing, so do it. Help us. Help buy time to get the little kids out of here."

Ignatius looked around, and for a moment, Luna thought that he might run again, but Luna could see that he was looking around to where Leon was still shepherding kids out of there.

"All right," Ignatius said. "All right, I'll help."

"Where are the vapor guns?" Luna asked.

"Still in the space we were using for a workshop," Ignatius replied. "I was using the original to help with replicas."

"Then we need to get there," Luna insisted. She looked back to see controlled bursting through the barricades. "Now, Ignatius!"

They ran for the caves, dodging past people without slowing down. One of the controlled came at Luna, and she ducked under his grab, continuing to run. They made it into the cave, not stopping as they ran for the space where Ignatius and Barnaby had been working. Bobby loped along at Luna's side, and she felt a lot safer with the dog's presence than she might have otherwise.

When they reached the workshop area, Barnaby was there, looking distraught as he tried to throw pieces of equipment into a bag.

"I don't know what to take," he said. "If we're going to find a real way to stop this, we'll need equipment, but I can't carry everything."

"Leave it," Luna said. "The materials lab will have plenty of equipment. Right now, the priority is helping people."

It said a lot about Barnaby that he didn't hesitate the way Ignatius had. "You're right. I'll help Leon get the others to safety."

Luna looked around, spotting one of the containers that they were using for Ignatius's vapor. "Wait. I have an idea. Do you have anything that we can get the vapor into? Jars, or balloons, or anything?"

"I'll find something," Barnaby promised.

Ignatius looked over at her. "You're planning to water bomb the controlled?"

"Won't it work?" Luna asked. She was worried that she might have misjudged how the vapor worked.

"I... guess it might," Ignatius said. "And then more than just a couple of people could use it. Yes, it has to be worth a try."

"You focus on getting the vapor guns," Luna said. "I'll help get jars and things."

She gathered what she could, all too aware that just outside, there were people fighting for their lives. Taking one of Ignatius's canisters of the vaccine, she started to siphon the vapor from it into jar after jar. Barnaby came back with his own jars, and with the balloons that Luna had suggested, filling them and putting them in the bag that he had been using for equipment.

"Right," Ignatius said, standing. He was carrying his vapor gun again, looking as though he was strapped into a combination of scuba gear and weed sprayer. Another one sat nearby, and Luna struggled her way into it. It was heavy for her, so that she had to concentrate on keeping her balance.

She strode out toward the entrance with the others in tow, and waded out into what looked like a full-scale battle. Luna saw a knot of the controlled descending on a group of the younger kids, and she made her way forward, hoping that the vapor gun would work just as well on them as it had on her and the others.

She sprayed them with the vapor, and they stopped, turning to her as if they might attack… then they collapsed, blinking as the vapor started to take effect. Luna passed makeshift water bombs to the kids.

"Here," she said. "Do you think you can throw these?"

They nodded, laughing and whooping as they flung them. The weapons burst as they hit, spraying liquid and vapor over the controlled and the Survivors alike. Luna saw the controlled pause, and then fall, twitching as the vaccine started to work. A few of the first ones she'd hit with the vapor were already groaning, starting to struggle back to their feet.

"There's no time to explain what's going on," she said. "Grab water bombs and hit some of the others."

Luna waded forward, still spraying the vapor. Bobby was with her, jumping up at any of the controlled who got too close, knocking them back long enough for the vapor to take effect. Around her, more and more people fell to the ground and slowly started to get up as themselves once more. She forced her way toward the canyon entrance, step by step.

"We're coming!" she yelled. "Hold on!"

The fighting there at the barricade was still intense. Of the bikers, the only one Luna could see was Cub, and she just had to hope that was because the others were hidden in the middle of the fight or had managed to escape. He was fighting alongside a knot of the survivors, and Luna used her spray gun to get closer to them, bringing down the controlled a few at a time.

"It's working," Ignatius yelled as he kept spraying the controlled. "We're actually winning this!"

To Luna's surprise, it looked as though he was right. More and more of the controlled were falling, and as they got up again, they joined in the fight. The vapor bombs were changing whole sections of the crowd back, so that it seemed that they might have the numbers now. Luna pushed her way forward, heading for Cub, changing the controlled as she went.

"Almost there," she called out, pushing her way next to him with Bobby's help. Cub was cut and bruised, blood spattering him from the fight. Luna saw controlled closing in on him, and sprayed them as quickly as she could. They stopped and fell.

She kept spraying as the controlled kept coming. There were fewer and fewer of them now, the last of the ones nearby staggering in, then collapsing.

They'd done it. They'd actually won a battle against the controlled.

"We won," Luna said, grabbing hold of Cub and dancing around him. She hugged him tight, and might have done more than that, but then she caught sight of his expression. "What is it? What happened?"

"The others... they charged out into the controlled. I think... I think they're gone."

Luna hugged him again, but this time it was about comfort, not celebration.

"Oh, Cub, I'm so sorry."

"I'm the last one left, and soon..."

And soon, he would be controlled, the same way Luna would be. The same way all the people they'd turned back would, eventually. Their only hope was to find a cure.

"We'll get to the laboratory," Luna said. "We'll find a way."

"We'll have to do it fast," Cub said.

Luna nodded. How long would it be now before they lost themselves again? She didn't know, and not knowing made it even worse than it was. She stared out into the distance, thinking about the laboratory that was out there, and the hope it held for all of them. If they could find the substance they needed, locate something that was just different enough from Ignatius's vapor, and maybe, just maybe, they had a hope.

"We still won today," she said.

Then Luna saw the dots in the sky, far away in the distance, and knew that the fight wasn't over.

"We need to get out of here," she said. "*Now.*"

She ran for the school bus they'd taken, with Cub and Bobby hurrying along beside her. Some of the Survivors and the people they'd changed back followed, running with them, probably hoping that Luna knew what she was doing.

They piled into the bus. Barnaby followed with some of the smallest children. Luna grabbed the wheel and managed to start it, the engine roaring into life while around them, others grabbed bikes or just ran. She got ready to leave, hoping she remembered enough about driving to be able to do it without crashing this time.

She saw Ignatius running for the bus, the chemist stumbling and getting tangled in his spray gun as he went.

"We need to go," Cub said.

Luna shook her head. "We need him. He saved me, he saved you, and he's our best chance for saving everyone."

Cub grimaced and then went to the door, holding out a hand, grabbing Ignatius as he came close and pulling him inside.

Luna set off driving, their armored school bus rumbling forward as the alien ships came into sight in the rearview mirror. She clung to the wheel with all her strength as she powered forward, and behind her, she saw the flicker of energy from the sky to the ground, the rising cloud of flame and smoke as shot after shot hit the Survivors' base. The roar of it filled the air, the heat rising up in a wall of fire that seemed to fill the world.

Luna kept driving. Their only hope now was to get to the laboratory.

CHAPTER SEVENTEEN

Ro felt… well, he felt *everything*. Happiness and sadness, joy and pain, fear, definitely fear at the thought that at any moment, the Hive might realize that he was disconnected, a rebel, no longer of the Purest but impure. Impure Ro.

Mostly, though, he felt guilt. There was guilt at having betrayed the Hive, although that was a reflex thing, not as strong as Ro might have imagined it would be, more fear than guilt. There was guilt at not feeling *more* guilt at his betrayal, and at every emotion he did feel.

The real washes of guilt, though, were reserved for the things Ro had done and helped to do. He had helped to attack worlds. He had helped to steal from them and transform their species, slaughtering what they did not change. Once, the fact that it had been for the good of the Hive had seemed like a sufficient excuse for all of it. Now, it didn't seem like even the beginnings of a justification.

He had helped to attack the Earth. He had helped to torment Chloe.

"Why her?" he asked himself. "Why does she matter more than all the rest?"

He knew the answer to that: because it had been her mind that had freed him, and her mind he had connected to so completely. He had been connected to all the other minds of the Hive in a general sense, had gone through the minds of hundreds, if not thousands, of creatures subjected to research, but it felt as though Chloe was a part of him now, some facet of her emotions swimming through him to wake up his own.

"I have to save her," he said, but that wasn't enough. He had to try to save all of them. He had to be the traitor to his people in his actions that he already was just in his existence. He had to find a way…

The boy, Kevin. Ro had seen what a weapon he was for the Hive. He could take the boy away from it. But for that, he would need Chloe.

He just hoped that he wasn't too late in getting to her.

He hurried through the flesh factories, disgust at all that was happening there rippling through him with every step. How could he have ever felt that this was right, or good, or even necessary? A part of him wanted to free every creature there, but a stronger part needed to get to Chloe, needed to help her.

He heard her screaming ahead and ran for the laboratory where he and the others had been getting ready to work on her, ignoring the need for propriety, or how seldom those of the Purest ever actually ran.

When he arrived, Purest Jir was standing over her, a bloody laser scalpel in its hand and a fluid metal leg nearby.

"I thought we agreed to wait for the results of the serum!" Ro demanded with more force than he would normally have said *anything*.

"Purest Ro, are you well?" Purest Jir asked. It gestured to where Chloe still hung in the air. "The serum is continuing to work on the girl, but I thought that one foot would not make a difference."

"You thought wrong!" Ro shouted.

"Purest Ro, you seem unwell. You seem almost to be exhibiting… traitorous thoughts. I shall summon assistance, and—"

Ro quickly scanned the laboratory's tables of instruments and tools, looking for something he could use. When his vision fell on a stunning rod usually used to subdue beasts for delicate work where their thrashing from pain would be inconvenient, he grabbed for it.

"What are you doing?" Purest Jir demanded. "I am a fellow member of the Purest, I am—"

"I've realized recently that you're someone I don't actually like very much," Ro said, before jabbing the rod into Purest Jir's flesh. It crackled, and his former colleague collapsed into insensibility.

"Are you all right?" Ro asked Chloe. "Did he hurt you?"

"What's going on?" Chloe demanded. "Is this some kind of trick? Wait… I didn't get anything from your translator. I can *understand* you?"

Ro quickly examined her. It seemed that Purest Jir had made an initial incision in her leg, but that was easy enough to seal with one of the devices the Hive had stolen from a species that valued healing above all else.

"It may be an effect of the connection that we made, or the serum that I gave you, or both," Ro said. "Wait a moment."

He picked up an auto injector, administering it to Chloe and wincing with her as she reacted to the pain.

"I am sorry," he said. "This will stop the progress of the serum inside you. It cannot undo any effects it has already had, and I do not know what those will be, but it will stop further changes."

"Why are you doing this?" Chloe demanded. "Is this some strange kind of test?"

"Wait, let me get you down from there," Ro said. He adjusted the gravity trap and let Chloe settle to what Ro considered to be the floor. She immediately ran over to the bench, grabbing an object with multiple points and prongs, holding it up in front of her as a weapon.

"Stay back," Chloe warned. "You were the one who injected me before!"

"I was," Ro agreed, and more guilt rose in him. "I am so sorry for what I have done."

Before, it would have seemed like an empty word, but now, Ro could see the point of it, and the meaning behind it: he was, literally, filled with sorrow at the thought that he had hurt Chloe.

"I was a part of the Hive," he explained, "and then... then I connected with your mind. I felt the emotions there, and I saw all that the Hive had cut itself off from. We pushed back emotions so that we would lose rage and violence and anger, but we lost love, and guilt, and compassion. I feel all of them again. I feel... so much."

Chloe looked over at him, and Ro guessed that there would be some kind of angry outburst from her. He had seen into her mind after all, and he knew the anger that lay there, and the reasons for it. Someone who had controlled her like this, who had treated her like this, would get no mercy.

Instead, she reached out to touch his arm.

"It's hard, isn't it, feeling too much?" she said.

Ro nodded, then looked down at the unconscious form of Purest Jir. "But it is *so* much better than the alternative." He looked over at the shock stick. "I do not know how long one of the Purest will be unconscious," he said. "We should go."

"We could kill it," Chloe said.

"*No*," Ro said, and his shock at it must have come through that. "No. To kill is... the thought of it feels wrong."

Chloe looked at him, then gave Purest Jir a kick. "I'm owed at least *that* much." She looked down at the symbiont on her arm. "Can you get this off me?"

"Not quickly," Ro said. "Possibly not safely. We need to go."

Chloe nodded and swapped her randomly grabbed piece of medical equipment for the shock stick.

"All right," she said, "but I still don't trust you. You stay where I can see you."

"Yes," Ro said.

111

He led the way from the laboratory, out into the flesh factories. He saw Chloe pale at the sight of the things going on there.

"We need to release them," she said.

"Some of them will be driven mad by the pain," Ro said. "They will be dangerous, and when Jir wakes up, the whole Hive will be seeking us."

"I don't care," Chloe snapped back. "If you can really feel things, then you can imagine what it's like for them."

"Pain," Ro said, "fear, helplessness." He hung his head. Chloe was right. He went to the first of the rooms, where creatures were being transformed in vats of viscous liquid. He reached for the controls, working them slowly, then changed his mind and stepped forward, tipping the vats over so that they tumbled out. They started to groan as Ro ripped them free of the devices holding them in place.

"Free the others," Ro said, when he was sure they could understand him. "This is your best chance. You need to free the next ones, and the next."

He could only hope that whatever conditioning they'd had to obey the Purest would help get the message across. Ro went across to another room, freeing another creature, then another.

"There are enough now that they will continue this on their own," Ro said.

"Will it be enough to stop the Hive?" Chloe demanded.

"I'm not sure that anything is enough to stop the Hive," Ro said. "Even now, they have used the boy you came with to attack another world."

"Kevin," Chloe said. "We have to save Kevin!"

"You know that he's at the heart of one of the spires?" Ro said. "And he is fully a part of the Hive now. To pull him out would take—"

"Exactly what it took with you," Chloe pointed out.

Ro couldn't argue with that. More to the point, he knew there was no point in arguing with *her*. He'd seen enough of Chloe's mind to know that she wouldn't leave without Kevin. Maybe grabbing Kevin was even a good thing. If the Hive needed him so much, then they could slow down the things it wanted to do. They could start to fight back.

"All right," Ro said. He grabbed the mental connection devices. "We will need these."

He led the way out through the city, on the long walk to the spire where the Hive told him that Kevin was. It was strange, being able to see it, yet not being a part of it. The crowds of creatures there parted, as they would for any of the Purest. It made Ro feel like a fraud and an imposter, but also grateful that they might be able to get to Kevin before the Hive rose to strike back at them.

"This way," he said, leading Chloe into the spire. "If anyone asks…"

He didn't have enough practice in lying to come up with a good suggestion.

"If anyone asks, it's important for the experiments that you connect me to Kevin," Chloe said, "and it might be bad for Kevin if you don't. They won't care enough about me to do it otherwise."

Ro nodded. He would never have been able to come up with all of that at once, but now that he heard it, he knew that the others would believe it. They would never consider the possibility that one of their own might lie.

He headed up through the building with Chloe until he reached the control space where Kevin stood with Purest Lux and a number of servitor creatures. Purest Lux turned to him as he arrived.

"What is this, Purest Ro?" Purest Lux demanded. "Why is the human female here?"

"Our work has demonstrated a potential problem, Purest Lux," Ro said, feeling fear as he did so. How did humans control these emotions? What would happen if Purest Lux worked out what was happening? What if their lie didn't work?

"What problem? Can it not wait, when we are in the middle of destroying an enemy?"

"I do not believe it can," Ro said. "Analysis of the girl has shown a potential instability in Kevin that must be normalized to prevent damage to him. We must connect their thoughts, and use her to stabilize him."

"Are you certain?" Purest Lux asked.

"Yes, Purest Lux," Ro said.

The pause after those words felt like the longest of Ro's life. It felt as though his lie would be discovered at any minute, and the servitor creatures would descend on them.

"Very well," Purest Lux said. "Do so at once."

"Kevin," Ro said, "permit me to place the devices on you."

He took out the mental connectors, letting their tentacles stick into place on Kevin's skull. He did the same with Chloe, remembering not to ask. He joined the connection too, partly to shield Purest Lux from it, and partly because he had experience of breaking free of the Hive's grasp.

Remember what it was to be human, he told Kevin, mind to mind. *Remember the emotions. Remember what you felt.*

What is this? Kevin replied. *Feelings are—*

Feelings are important! Chloe sent across to him. *They make you human. They make you Kevin.*

Ro pulled mentally at the connections between Kevin and the Hive, stretching them, weakening them. *I know that you can feel, Kevin. I know that you want to. Fight what we did to you. Remember why you came here.*

Please, Kevin, Chloe put in. *Please. I know the real Kevin is in there somewhere. The Kevin I know. The Kevin I... love.*

Ro could feel the waves of emotion that came with that, stronger than anything he could have produced. He could feel them washing over the connections that bound Kevin to the Hive, feel them starting to transform things.

He felt the moment when those connections snapped, and heard Kevin gasp, back in the real world.

"Is everything all right?" Purest Lux asked.

Purest Ro had to make up his own lie this time. "I believe the experience of correcting the problem has been quite strenuous for Kevin," he said. "With your permission, I would like to take him to a medical bay to run tests."

"Very well," Purest Lux said. "Return to your experiments on the human female when you are done. I am told that Purest Jir was planning some most intriguing alterations to it."

"Yes, Purest Lux," Ro said. He put his hands on the backs of Kevin and Chloe, guiding them in the direction of the door and walking as fast as he dared. If they could just get out of there, they would be fine, but it would only take one moment in which Purest Lux wondered too much about Purest Jir's experiments, and realized through the Hive that he was unconscious, one moment where Purest Jir recovered, and—

As if wishing for the moment had brought it, Ro heard the blare of Purest Jir's mind through the Hive, yelling loud enough for all to hear in a space where such things shouldn't have applied.

Help, Purest Ro is a traitor! It attacked me and stole the girl! Do not trust it, or anything that it says!

Ro looked around, seeing the servitor creatures shifting in their seats, clearly not knowing how to react to the news. Purest Lux stood there, apparently trying to work out the precise implications of everything that Purest Jir had just sent. For a moment, just a moment, the control room door was still clear, and there was only one thing to do.

"Run!" Ro shouted to the others, pushing them forward.

CHAPTER EIGHTEEN

Kevin ran on instinct, but a part of him could barely remember how to, he was so overwhelmed with emotion right then. He could remember everything that had happened while he'd been a member of the Hive, everything that he'd *done*. He'd helped to bring down the shields of the world below, he'd helped to attack its inhabitants...

...he'd sent Chloe away to die.

"Chloe... I..." he began.

"Keep running!" she yelled back as they hurried through the spire. "This is no time to tell me what you're feeling!"

"Feelings are important," the Purest running with them said. "They fill the world. They pervade everything. They—"

"*You* keep running too, Ro," Chloe yelled at him.

They ran, and Kevin could hear footsteps behind them, sounding far too loud against the metal of the spire's floors. Kevin was just glad that the Hive didn't keep the worst of its killer beasts in the spires, and that the servitors chasing them were better suited to tasks requiring strength or obedience than to speed.

They reached a curving ramp that lead through the interior like a staircase. The only question now was which way to go.

"Do we go up or down?" Kevin yelled. He couldn't think straight. He was still thinking about all the evil things that he'd done while he'd been a member of the Hive. He hadn't chosen it. He'd said no to it. He'd said no, and they had still convinced him to become one of them.

"Focus, Kevin," Chloe said, and then shook her head with a smile. "Things must be pretty bad if I'm the only one holding things together."

"That's because you're amazing," Kevin said. After everything Chloe had been through on the alien's world ship, she was still there, still able to think of what to do next. They still needed to decide which way to run, but that decision was made for them when Kevin heard the chittering sound of far more dangerous things approaching from below, coming up the ramp with frightening speed.

"Up!" Kevin yelled. "We need to go up!"

They started off up the ramp, running as fast as they could. It was hard. Now that he wasn't a part of the Hive anymore, Kevin could feel his body straining with the effort of staying ahead of the things chasing them. He just hoped that there would be a door soon, or something they could put between them, or something they could use to fight.

Instead, they came out onto the roof of the spire.

There *was* a door there behind them, and Kevin sealed it quickly, hoping it would hold against everything that was chasing them. Above, the power source at the heart of the world ship glowed with white hot malignancy, ready to fire on the alien planet below it. Around them, all of the golden spires crackled with power as they controlled it, directing it.

"We have to find some way to stop this," Kevin said, staring up at it in horror. "We can't just let them destroy a whole *planet*."

He saw Chloe nod. "If there's a way—"

"There is no way," Ro said. "With the process this far along, and outside of the control rooms..." He shook his head. "It cannot be stopped."

Behind them, Kevin heard something start to bang on the doors.

"There has to be *something*," Kevin insisted. There was already so much on his conscience. He couldn't be responsible for the destruction of a whole planet too. He had to help *somehow*.

"The most I can hope to do is to distract the Hive through my connection to it," Ro said. "It will not stop the destruction, but at least it might give some a chance to get away."

The banging on the doors was getting louder now, the golden metal buckling under the impact of something far stronger than anything human.

"Do it," Kevin said.

Ro nodded, and seemed to concentrate, his white eyes screwing up with the effort of it. He went still, in an almost trancelike state, and Kevin wished he could see what was going on in the Hive, but his own connection seemed to have been cut more completely, or perhaps it was just that he wasn't one of the Purest.

"They're pushing back against me," he said. "I don't know what will confuse them most."

"Emotion," Chloe said. "They don't understand it."

Ro nodded. Kevin was more worried about the thuds that continued to come from the golden door behind them.

"I... think... I have... it..." Ro managed, but he didn't open his eyes; didn't make any move to continue their escape.

"We still need to get out of here," Kevin said.

"I don't think I can move," Ro replied. "I can hold it, but I must... concentrate."

"So we're just supposed to *abandon* you?" Chloe demanded. She didn't sound happy about that prospect.

Kevin couldn't see what other options there were, though, with the banging growing louder on the door and the alien unable to move. If they stood there with him, they would all die soon. If Ro ran, then so many others would be killed as the Hive picked off anyone trying to run from the world below.

Then he saw the golden disc on the floor and had an idea.

"Help Ro onto that disc," he said, and he and Chloe each took one of the Purest's arms, helping him aboard. "Ro, do you have a controller for the disc?"

"Chloe's... symbiont..."

Kevin didn't understand for a moment, but then, staring at the thing on Chloe's arm, he realized that it was the same as the thing the Purest had used to control the gravity around them. It was a connection to the gravity systems of the ship, and probably far more.

"Chloe," he said. "This disc can fly, and you have the controls for it. Press the thing on your arm and see what happens."

"What if it bites my arm off?" Chloe replied.

At that moment, the golden doors to the roof gave way, and creatures poured out. They were horrifying, looking part ape, part wolf, part insect. One surged forward, and Kevin acted on instinct, grabbing the stun stick out of Chloe's hand and jabbing it at the thing. The beast gave a shriek and reared back as energy crackled into it, and Kevin hit it again.

"Now, Chloe!" he yelled, and felt the golden disc jerk into the air unsteadily.

"I don't know what I'm doing!" Chloe yelled back.

"So long as it keeps us out of reach of those things and lets Ro concentrate, it's fine," Kevin said. He kept a hand on the alien, steadying him although the disc's own gravity meant it was probably nearly impossible to fall off. In the other hand, he held the shock stick ready.

Kevin saw her press at the thing on her arm, making a disgusted face every time she touched it. The disc spun left, then right, lifted up and dropped down.

"I think I've got it," Chloe said.

It looked as though it was just in time, because at least another couple of the golden discs were rising up over the city around them, surrounded by buzzing things that looked part alive, part mechanical, like giant clockwork wasps.

"We need to get out of here," Kevin called out as the things came at them.

Chloe seemed to get the message, because their golden disc set off through the air at a frightening pace, zipping low to the ground and then rising up again, shooting past gray buildings and through tangles of wires.

The chasers followed them. One of the wasp things came close, jabbing out with a stinger that sprayed a noxious green substance. Kevin jabbed back with his stun rod, and the thing tumbled from the sky to the ground below. Another followed close, zipping after them and looking for a chance to attack. Kevin circled around with it until it was in front of him, just hovering ahead and waiting to come in.

He ducked as Chloe took them under a bridge, dragging Ro down with him. The wasp thing wasn't so quick, and struck against it in a shower of green liquid. It burned when Kevin touched it.

"Ow!" he said.

"You shouldn't touch things that come out of giant poisonous wasps then," Chloe said.

"There are still more of them," Kevin said, pointing back.

"There will always be more," Ro managed from where he stood. "The Hive has a whole world of servitors."

"Then we need to get *off* this world," Kevin said, looking around until he found one of the spaces that had served to let ships out into the atmosphere around the planet. "There. If we can get to it, there might still be a ship."

"Because that worked out *so* well last time," Chloe muttered, but she still set off in the direction of the hangar, and whatever might lie inside it.

The others chased them. The golden platforms came closer, like boats bobbing on a river, ready for boarding. One of the Purest stood on each, along with servitor creatures who had guns that fired bursts of energy that flew through the air, missing their platform and slamming into the interior surface of the world ship.

"Hold on!" Chloe yelled, as the golden disc zigged and zagged, dodging the worst of the blasts. The strangest thing was that there was no need to hold on; the disc's gravity kept them all firmly in place even when they looped and rolled. It also meant that the enemies on other discs were just as firmly fixed to their discs.

One leapt across, and Kevin zapped it with the stun stick. He held it like a sword, ready to thrust at any enemy who came too close, but it wasn't as though he could scare any member of the Hive off. It wasn't as though they felt fear. More leapt, and even though they fell tumbling to the ground when Kevin hit them with the stun stick, they didn't seem to care. As long as the Purest continued to pilot them…

"If that's what it takes," Kevin said to himself, and stood ready for the next time one of the golden discs came close.

He didn't wait for the creatures aboard to try to board them this time. Instead, *he* boarded *their* golden disc, leaping over with a shout and charging straight at the Purest piloting the thing. Kevin pushed past a couple of the servitor creatures in the way, darting around questing claws as he lunged forward to drive the shock stick straight into the Purest.

Instantly, Kevin turned and ran, his foot reaching the edge of the golden disc as it faltered and fell. He leapt, his legs continuing to run in the air, his arms pinwheeling. He managed to catch the edge of the disc, almost sliding off the edge as he tried to keep hold of the shock stick. He clamped his teeth together as he struggled to pull himself up, throwing one leg up toward the edge and managing to catch a foot on it. Kevin rolled onto his back, and would have lain there panting except that one of the wasp things flew in close. Kevin sat up, jabbing the shock stick at it, and struggled back to his feet as it fell.

"Don't you dare," Chloe said as he readied himself to take a leap at the second disc. "You almost died with the last one."

She pulled the disc back away from the second one, and Kevin stopped short of the edge. Instead of jumping, he weighed the shock stick in his hand. He threw it, and the stick tumbled end over end, striking the Purest on the second disc in a shower of sparks and sending the disc tumbling downward.

Their disc shot forward toward the hangar, leaving their pursuers behind. It wouldn't buy them much time, but maybe the little it had given them would be enough. They shot into the hangar, which seemed mostly empty, like a bird roost without birds. Some of the smaller hunter ships hung there, much sleeker and more dangerous looking than the one that had brought them there. Kevin could feel his excitement building a little at the thought of being able to actually *fly* one of them.

Chloe landed the golden disc beside one of the nearest ones, and they took one of Ro's arms each, helping him off as he shook and swayed, his eyes tightly shut in concentration. He was big enough and tall enough that it took both of them to guide him through the doors of the alien fighter, closing them after themselves and locking them shut.

From the windows, Kevin saw aliens advancing toward their chosen ship. There was nowhere to run now. If they got there, then Kevin, Chloe, and Ro would be caught and killed with no way out. They *had* to get off of the world ship.

"Ro, can you help us get this thing flying?" Kevin asked, but the alien didn't respond. Instead, he stood there in what looked like grim concentration. Kevin guessed they wouldn't be able to snap him out of that quickly, and that even if they somehow did, it would be a bad thing, since the Hive would be able to see them and strike at them as they ran, along with all the refugees from the world below.

He moved to the cockpit of the ship, trying to work out how it ran. He'd seen through the eyes of pilots, sent instructions down to a fleet of craft like this, and he *thought* he knew how they worked, but that had been when they were already flying, not when they were just hanging there.

"We have to get this ship going," Kevin said.

"I know," Chloe replied. "I'm trying."

She had the thing on her arm pressed against the ship's control panel, and Kevin could hear the hum of power that was coming from it. There seemed to be a connection there, the same way that there had been with the golden disc, and now Kevin could see the controls lighting up.

He could also hear things banging on the doors.

Reaching out, he grabbed for what he hoped were the right controls. He grasped a kind of joystick, and a big throttle control that looked like a lever to push forward. He accelerated the ship, its drives pushing it away from the clamps that held it so that they squealed in protest. Kevin felt something give… and then they were bursting away from the ship.

They moved away from the docking section of the world ship, out through the shield that kept its air inside. Kevin twisted the ship gently to make it fit, and then, with no break between, they were out in space, blackness surrounding them.

He was flying. He was actually flying.

Carefully, Kevin guided the ship away from the world ship, moving slowly and carefully, not daring to go any faster. He looped away from its misshapen surface, seeing the crackle of energy building up on it. He did his best to open a radio channel, hoping he could remember the right buttons to make it work.

"If there's anyone listening, you need to get away from the surface of the world," he warned. "They're going to use some kind of weapon on it. They're going to blow it up!"

Something moved into sight: one of the sleek forms of the defenders' ships. Kevin recognized it for what it was even as he realized that it was flying straight for him.

"No," he called out over the radio. "We're not planning to attack you. We're *escaping*. We broke free of the—"

A blast of light cut him off, and something ripped through the ship, sending Kevin sprawling.

CHAPTER NINETEEN

Luna drove the bus forward, feeling every jolt in the road, punctuated by occasional bigger jolts as they hit abandoned cars, the snowplow shoving them out of the way. Luna had to fight to keep hold of the wheel, the driver's seat all the way forward, determined that *she* was going to be the one to get them to their destination. Beside her, Bobby leaned into her, pretty much holding her in place with his weight.

"They're gone," Cub said, sitting on the seat nearest to the driver's. He didn't look up. "They're all gone."

Luna could understand that kind of sense of loss now. She knew what it was like to lose friends, and family, and everyone else she'd ever known. Everyone knew what that felt like now, and it *hurt*. It was the worst feeling in the world.

"That's part of what we're fighting to get back," Luna said. "We can still save so many people."

"Not the ones who have died though," Cub said. "Not my dad."

Luna understood how that hurt too. Even if they found a permanent cure today, there would still be some people it wouldn't help. So many people had died for real, not just been controlled by the aliens.

"Maybe not us either," Cub said. "Not unless we're quick."

Luna looked over at him, ignoring the jolt that came from a parked car. Bobby barked.

"You're not turning back controlled, are you?" she asked. She didn't know what she would do if the answer was yes. Cub was one of the coolest people she'd met, and he liked her, and she... well, she liked him too. She wasn't sure she could stop the bus and force him off to walk out into LA. She *definitely* couldn't try to kill him.

"Not yet," Cub said, "but I can feel it building up in me. It's like a kind of pressure, and it's always there, whatever I do. Can't you feel it?"

"I can," Luna admitted. The fear of turning back was always just under the surface, and the threat of it was there too. Like Cub said, it was like a pressure inside of her, the part controlled by the aliens ready to come bursting to the surface if she didn't fight it every—

They slammed into another car, the jolt pulling Luna from her thoughts. It would have knocked her from her seat too if Bobby hadn't pushed into her, holding her in place.

"Careful!" Ignatius called out from further down the bus.

"You should be up here anyway," Luna said. "You're the one who says we should try the materials lab. You need to help find the way."

"UCLA isn't hard to find," Ignatius said.

Maybe that was true normally. In a city like LA, maybe broad streets and big landmarks made it hard to get lost, but that was without the chaos that had come from the aliens' landing. There were so many cars abandoned in the streets now that even with the modified bus, it was getting harder to push through. Buildings, meanwhile, had been picked clean by looters, either the controlled or just people trying to take what they could from the chaos.

The bus traveled slowly, but that was fine, because at least it meant that some of the other Survivors could keep up with them on their bikes, the engines sounding higher and faster against the dull note of the bus. It formed the head of a kind of convoy, moving through LA at only a little more than walking pace, bikes following in its wake, and a stumbling, shuffling mass of refugees from the Survivors' base following in theirs.

"We won't be able to go back," Luna said. "Not with everything the aliens did there."

The energy blasts looked as though they had utterly destroyed the Survivors' home. The scale of the blast said that the aliens had been serious about wiping out any attempt by humanity to live on past the invasion of their world.

Or maybe it said something that held more hope. Maybe it said that Luna and the others were on the right track. The aliens wouldn't keep trying to kill Ignatius if they weren't scared that his formula was close to something that could stop them, would they? They wouldn't put so much effort into it, at least not if they knew that everyone turned back would become one of the controlled again in less than a week.

"That way," Ignatius said, pointing.

Luna did her best to follow the chemist's directions, although he didn't seem to understand the scale of some of the obstacles in the way. A sign lay on its side, neon still flickering as it blocked the road. A food truck had been dragged into the middle of the street, opened up by blowtorches like a can whose contents people were desperate to get at. The food would be running out by now, Luna realized. Even the people who weren't controlled would be desperate.

Some of the obstacles were too big for the bus alone. More than a couple of cars, and it simply didn't have the power to shove them out of the way. Luna felt the bus snarl and stall as she shoved it into a cluster of vehicles, pushing like an angry bull but unable to make any progress.

"We're stuck," she yelled.

A dozen of the Survivors got off the bus to help with it, filing out and starting to push and pull at the cars. That was nothing compared to the numbers who came forward from the crowd of refugees behind them, helping even though they were no longer strong, no longer incapable of feeling tiredness or pain.

Luna got down from the bus and moved beyond the blockage, looking for a way through. She saw a flicker of movement in one of the nearby buildings, and tensed herself to fight, yet what she saw was a girl who looked even younger than she did, looking out at them with obvious fear.

"Hey," Luna called. "You don't have to be afraid. My name's Luna. What's yours?"

The girl darted back into the building, and maybe the sensible thing to do was to leave her there, but that felt far too much like abandoning someone they might be able to help, and right then, Luna wanted to feel as though she was helping everyone she could before the aliens' vapor claimed her. Besides, it would take at least another few minutes before the armored bus was free, and the way Luna saw it, she could spend that time standing there pushing, or she could do something that was actually *useful*.

She set off following the girl. If it had been anyone other than a girl like her, she probably wouldn't have done it. Luna had seen firsthand just how desperate the world had made some people. Yet the girl there had looked so scared in the brief instant that Luna had seen her, and something in Luna wanted to be able to help her as she darted into the nearest building after her, and...

There, another flicker of movement.

"I'm not here to hurt you," she said. "You've seen how many people we have outside. I want to *help* you."

She moved a little deeper into the building. Not far; just enough to try to find the girl. She came out into a large room, and there were half a dozen men waiting there, all dangerous looking and dressed in well-worn clothes that they'd obviously been rooting around in the ruins of LA in. The girl stood among them, gesturing back to Luna.

124

"There, I *told* you I'd bring you a good one," she said. "So our debt's cleared, right? Right, Vern? You'll let me go?"

"Shut up," one of the men said.

He started to step toward Luna, and Luna didn't wait. She turned and ran. Anything that men like this wanted to lure people here for wouldn't be good. Talking about "a good one" just made it worse. She sprinted for the way out as fast as she could.

The girl with them was faster, running after Luna and diving at her, grabbing her ankle so that Luna stumbled.

"No you don't!" the girl shouted. "If they don't sell you, then they'll sell *me*, and—"

Luna kicked her in the face, breaking free, all pity gone after the way she'd tricked her.

Then the man, Vern, was there, a gun in his hand, raised in a threat.

"Try to run again and I'll shoot you in the leg. The people who'll buy you don't need you to be able to walk."

Luna raised her hands, trying not to think about the times that she'd had guns pointed at her in the past...

Bobby growled and leapt at the man, biting his arm hard.

The gun clattered to the floor, and Luna was away running again, Bobby running at her side. She heard the sound of booted feet behind her, followed by shots, and she made sure that she never ran in a straight line for more than a few paces. Shots pinged off the walls, and she knew she'd done the right thing. She heard a cry behind her, and suspected that it might be the other girl, but Luna kept going. She'd already tried to help her, and look where that had gotten her.

She heard the sound of people ahead, and ran for them. Behind her, the footsteps kept coming, but Luna didn't care. She just had to—

"Got you!" Vern said, grabbing hold of her. Luna tried to kick her way free, but the bigger man just lifted her off the floor so that her foot didn't connect properly.

"Help!" Luna called out.

"No one's going to care," Vern said as she shouted. "This is a big, bad world. All the governments are gone. The aliens' world is gone. It's just us, and what we can take."

"We care," a voice from further along said.

Luna looked over and sighed with relief. Leon was there, and Ignatius, and about a dozen of the other members of the Survivors, armed with guns. Cub was there too, looking on with obvious anger.

"Didn't you see us coming through?" Luna said. "Or were you too busy hiding away, hoping your bait would bring people to you?"

"I could still kill you," Vern said, stepping back and pointing his gun at her. He'd obviously retrieved it from the floor before running after her.

Luna's mind flashed back to thoughts of the crazy guy at the press conference. This time, she wasn't just going to stand there and be a victim. This time, she was in control of things.

"You have one chance to keep living, Vern," she said. "You can put that gun down, turn around, and run fast enough that when my people come after you, they don't catch you. Otherwise, when I count to three, they're going to shoot you, and I'm going to take my chances. I don't think you'll be able to fire before all of them, personally."

"You think I won't do it?" he demanded. "You think I won't shoot you?"

Luna shrugged. "One... two..."

He threw down his gun and ran. Luna was... not exactly content to let a man like that go, but was at least glad that he *was* going. She turned back to the others.

"So," Leon said. "We're your people, are we?"

"Yes," Luna said with a sigh of relief. "Yes you are."

***

They kept going deeper into the city, and now Luna caught flickers of movement among the broken-open stores and the empty houses. No one attacked them now, but she had the feeling that if there hadn't been so many of them, then they might have been. It frustrated her a little that people might revert to that kind of thing the moment the situation got hard. The coming of the aliens had changed even those people they hadn't succeeded in transforming with their vapor.

"Come down!" she yelled up to them, Bobby at her side. "Come and help us win this! Don't you want your world back? Don't you want to fight?"

There was no answer from above. Maybe they were too scared to come down. Maybe they just didn't care. Luna hated the thought that, even at the end of the world, there might still be people out there who weren't prepared to help one another.

All their convoy could do was keep going, and hope they would be able to make the world better for everyone. They pushed

126

through the streets, moving obstacles out of the way or driving around them, heading for the university's campus.

As they reached it, Luna tried to imagine what it would be like in normal times. The buildings there were big and varied, obviously built to different tastes at different times. There were plenty of open spaces between them, although now those were starting to get overgrown with weeds.

Luna pulled the bus up right in the middle of one of the main plazas, not caring that normally it wouldn't have been allowed. They needed to be as close to it as they could get if they had to run again. She really *hoped* they didn't have to run again. She got out with Bobby next to her, and the others started to gather around. Leon and Barnaby gathered with the other Survivors; Ignatius was further away. Cub had decided to stand with the people they had turned back from the controlled into humans.

"We need to find the materials labs," she said, trying to sound confident that she would know what those looked like when she saw them. "We're looking for a very specific substance." She looked around at Ignatius. "How will we recognize it?"

"I can identify it," Ignatius said, "and so can Barnaby. If we get it under a microscope or into a spectrometer, we'll know it."

"So we have to go through every single sample a university possesses until we find the right thing?" Luna said. She was no expert, but she was pretty sure that somewhere with a whole lab full of different materials would take a while to search.

"Unless you have a better idea?" Ignatius said.

Luna didn't, which meant that they had to get started. She looked around until she found a signpost, and while Bobby stood sniffing it, she picked out the direction of the materials laboratories.

"This way!" she called to the others.

She could make out the building now, dark and empty like so many of the others, modern and silent as their group made their way over to it. The doors were locked, but with so many of them there, it was an easy thing to pick up a bench to use as a battering ram.

"Ready?" Luna called. "One, two, three!"

They smashed their way inside, and Luna picked her way through the debris with Bobby, ahead of the others.

"We need to spread out," she said. "Find anything that's different, or isn't clearly labeled, or... I don't know, just see what you can find."

She knew it was too general, but what else could she do? They had to start somewhere, so she set off searching with the others, picking a room and starting to go through the materials there in search of the one that they wanted.

The problem wasn't finding things, it was that there were far too *many* things that she could find. Even a minute of searching revealed a hundred different glass slides, each presumably containing a sample of some kind of substance. Luna took all of them across to the lab where Ignatius and Barnaby were already starting to look through microscopes at possible samples.

"No," Ignatius said. "Not that one... not that one either..."

"I have more," Luna said, running in with Bobby close behind her. "Maybe it's one of these."

"We don't need *more*," Ignatius said. "There are too many to identify as it is."

Luna shrugged. "So it will take a while. For a way to stop all of this, it's worth it."

Ignatius shook his head. "It won't take 'a while.' For the number of samples there are in here, we're looking at weeks. That's too long."

Luna wanted to argue with that, wanted to tell Ignatius to just keep working, but she knew he had a point. They didn't have the kind of time it would take to find what they were looking for. *She* didn't have that much time. By the time they had found it, all of the people helping them would have reverted to being controlled, and so would she. And that was only if the aliens didn't destroy the world outright.

"What do you have in mind?" Luna asked.

"There will be a system for cataloguing samples," Ignatius said. "If we just fire that up—"

"No," Luna said, thinking of the NASA institute. "You don't know what that will do."

She could remember what it had been like, with the controlled fighting to get in, having to run desperately, barely making it out in time.

"There has to be another way," she said.

Ignatius shook his head. "Not that I can see, and I *do* know what will happen. The moment we connect any kind of signal, the aliens will spot where we are. They'll come here in force."

"But we can be prepared," Barnaby said. He sighed. "I think that's our best chance, Luna. Ignatius is right: we'll never get through all of these samples in time by hand. We can tell the others, give them time to hide or build barricades."

Luna hated the idea of having to do things that way. She had seen what it could be like when the aliens came. So had everyone else, though. The Survivors had all been there when the aliens attacked their home. Ignatius had been followed by the aliens wherever they could find him. The people who had been controlled... well, they knew better than anyone what could happen.

"All right," she said. "But anyone who wants to leave gets to leave."

"Including me?" Ignatius asked.

Luna fixed him with a stare. "Would you really leave when there was a chance to end this?"

Ignatius stood there for a moment or two. Then he sighed. "No, I guess not."

"Okay," Barnaby said. "I'll tell Leon and the others."

***

Luna hit at nails with a hammer, trying to make sure that the barricade they were building would hold together. Around her, dozens of other people worked with her, bringing out furniture and heavy pieces of equipment with which to build obstacles. The ones with weapons, from the dart and vapor guns to the real kind, sat working on them, getting them ready. Bobby sat by Luna's feet, looking out as if he would guard her from whatever was coming.

Barnaby came up. "Leon says that if we're doing this, we should do it now, before it gets dark."

That made a kind of sense. Facing aliens was bad enough. Facing them in the dark, when they could come from any angle and looked just like people... that thought was too horrifying for words.

"Okay," Luna said. "Show me where we're doing this."

Barnaby led the way inside, and Luna followed. Ignatius sat there in front of a computer that was currently blank, no power running to it.

"Once I start to power this up, they'll know someone is here," he said. "Once they see what I'm searching for..."

They would come with everything they had. Or maybe they wouldn't. Maybe they would be lucky, and the aliens would miss what they were doing. Luna knew that they couldn't trust that to happen, though.

"Be as quick as you can," Luna said.

Ignatius nodded, and then powered up the computer.

"Okay, it's booting up and logging in. Open access. We need a search engine for materials. Come *on,* why don't academics ever put things in a sensible *order*?"

Silently, Luna found herself counting the seconds, her hand buried in Bobby's fur for reassurance.

"I'm into something called ChemFind," Ignatius said. "Now to describe the molecular structure…"

"Work quickly," Luna said. The seconds kept ticking away in her head.

"This isn't *easy*, you know," Ignatius said. His fingers tapped away at the keyboard, each movement seeming too slow, seeming to take too long.

"We need to stop before they see us," Barnaby said.

"Almost got it," Ignatius said.

"We need to stop," Barnaby repeated.

"Almost… *there*. I've found it!" Ignatius looked almost surprised. So surprised that he didn't seem to think to shut the computer down. Luna did though. She darted forward and pressed the shutdown button, hoping that it would be in time.

"Where?" Luna asked. "Where *is* it, Ignatius?"

"There's a meteorite museum on campus, full of samples people have collected over the years," the chemist said. "We want sample 542/R."

"Then let's go," Luna said.

She didn't wait for the others, but instead ran across in the direction of UCLA's meteorite museum, Bobby keeping step with her as she ran.

"Sample 542/R!" she yelled as she passed Cub. "We have to find sample 542/R!"

Cub ran with her, and they headed into the museum, past exhibit after exhibit that consisted of carefully displayed rocks. If Kevin's meteorite had proved to be what the aliens had claimed, would it have ended up here? There was no time to think about that; they had to find the right sample.

Even with the sample number, it wasn't easy, because there were so many different exhibits. Many of them were just the meteorites, with plaques saying who had found them, where, and when. Some had clusters of crystals beside them, or metal samples, representing some unusual composition. To Luna, it all just looked like rocks.

They headed up onto the next floor, looking at more samples that gave no clue as to why they should be up there and not downstairs with the others. Luna risked a glance out of one of the windows, and saw the people below standing ready at the barricades. They had to get this done soon, or—

"I found it!" Cub called out. "Here! 542/R!"

Luna ran over, half expecting the rock in the exhibit to be glowing. Instead, it was blue-gray, maybe a little larger than a football, with a collection of grown crystals down beside it.

"This is one of a collection of meteorites that fell to earth in the 1920s," Luna read from the plaque. "The mineral composition appears unusual." She laughed to herself. "You can say that again, card writing person." She looked around for a way to open the case, found that it was locked, and picked up a fire extinguisher. "Here goes nothing."

She hit the case and it shattered in a way that would probably have triggered an alarm if the whole building hadn't been powered down. As it was, glass crashed and crunched as it hit the floor, leaving the meteorite there on its stand.

"We did it," Luna said, joyously. "We did it."

"We did," Cub said with a tight smile. "There's just one problem."

"What?" Luna asked, and Cub pointed to the window. Luna looked out and saw them.

There were more than there had been at the Survivors' base, far more. Worse, there weren't just the controlled out there. Alien ships flew in, hovering just a short way above the ground. Where they stopped, things dropped down that reminded Luna far too much of the things that had been in the storm sewers. They moved forward on too many legs, trampling the controlled who got in their way.

"We've left it too late," Cub said. "We're surrounded!"

CHAPTER TWENTY

Kevin was at school. He wasn't sure how he was back at school, but right then, nothing much made sense. The world seemed to spin, and he managed to stumble his way to his feet.

"Kevin McKenzie, what are you doing?" his teacher called out.

"I…" Kevin shook his head. "I was on a spaceship. The Hive… we'd escaped the Hive…"

He tried to remember, but his head hurt so much now.

"Kevin, you're interrupting the lesson. There's no time for more of your alien nonsense."

"Kevin sees aliens. Kevin sees aliens," his classmates chanted.

No, this wasn't right. It didn't happen like this. It hadn't happened like this. He only learned about the Hive later…

"Kevin, are you all right?" his teacher asked.

Kevin tried to tell him that he was fine, but the only thing that came out was a spill of numbers in an endless stream that filled the world. The numbers spilled out from him and into his classmates, and now they were chanting the numbers, making them sound like a taunt even as they fell into step with one another.

No, this wasn't right, either. It hadn't happened like this; none of it had.

"Right, we're taking you to the principal," the teacher said.

They marched down corridors that Kevin remembered from the NASA institute, in the direction of a spot he recognized as Professor Brewster's office. The doors along the way opened in response to the stream of numbers spilling from him, although his mother looked at him sternly every time he spoke. When had it gone from his teacher to his mother leading him?

The door to Professor Brewster's office was open now, but the scientist wasn't within. Instead, Purest Lux was there, along with a blade-limbed creature in surgical scrubs.

"Ah, Kevin," it said. "I see that you have been disrupting lessons again. We will have to do something about that. Are you feeling unwell?"

Kevin wanted to say that he felt fine, but he didn't. Right then, it was as though every symptom that he'd ever have was there at once, his head pounding, his balance nonexistent, pain and weakness shooting through his body.

"We can make all of it go away," Purest Lux assured him. The alien gestured, and the nurse with the blades for hands came forward while the world continued to shift, and whirl, and spin...

***

The ship spun uncontrollably, and as he came back to himself, Kevin spun with it, floating free in the confines of its cockpit. He tumbled, weightless, and both Chloe and Ro tumbled around him, Chloe struggling for whatever grip she could find, Ro screaming out in obvious, uncontrollable fear.

"I do not like *this* emotion!" Ro called out.

Kevin tried to imagine what it would be like to have never felt fear before, or hope, or any other emotion. Even though he'd felt the blank logic of the Hive, it wasn't the same for him, because he'd had all the time growing up to get the hang of emotions, at least in theory. He couldn't begin to imagine what it would be like for someone who didn't know what fear was like, or who had never believed that they were going to die before.

Kevin was scared too, of everything that was happening, of the great world ship outside, of the smaller ship that had shot at them, but he'd spent far too much time already being sure he was going to die to be paralyzed by the fear now.

"We have to stop spinning!" he yelled.

He reached out his arms until he could make contact with the walls, and pushed off them like a swimmer in the direction of the pilot's chair. He managed to pull himself into it, strapping himself in and reaching out a hand for Chloe as she floated past. She grabbed for him, and Kevin's fingers closed around hers as he pulled her in close enough that she could grab hold of the pilot's console.

"Ro next," Kevin said, waiting until the alien was in reach.

"Ro, hold out your hands," Chloe shouted.

"I don't think I can. It's all so frightening. There's so much that—"

"It's okay to be scared," Chloe said. "It's okay to feel all kinds of things, but you can't panic, or you'll make it worse. You still have to do things. You have to trust people. The *right* people. Hold out your hands, Ro."

The alien floated a moment longer, then stretched out his arms toward them. Kevin was able to grab one, and Chloe the other, pulling him in to grab hold of the seat.

"Ro, I need you to tell me how to stop the ship spinning," Kevin said. "We're out of control."

"I…" The alien appeared to think for a moment. "The joystick controls might still be functioning. If we can level out, we can see how bad the damage is."

Kevin reached for the joystick, wrestling with it in an effort to get the ship back on a level course. The stars spun around him, fast enough that they were blurs as the ship continued to spiral. Kevin hauled on the stick, throwing his weight onto it as he willed it to stop spinning. Chloe lent her weight to it too, her hands wrapping over Kevin's, even though it left her floating again.

Slowly, though, the ship leveled out, the planet visible ahead of them, the Hive's world ship visible above, glowing with a blaze of energy. Kevin had to fight the way the ship wanted to go into a roll in the other direction, holding it there as steadily as he could.

"The loss of gravity means that our internal shield is damaged," Ro said. "We need to reboot it, or we will lose all of our oxygen." A look of what Kevin guessed was terror crossed his face. "We're going to die. We're—"

"We're going to *fix* this," Kevin insisted. "Chloe, can you fly the ship? Ro, you need to show me how to restart the shield like you said."

He released himself from the chair as Chloe clambered in, taking the joystick and setting the ship wobbling.

"Hey, this is fun," she said. "Trucks, boats, and now spaceships. I'm running out of things to drive."

"She makes jokes because she is scared," Ro said, as Kevin floated over in his direction. "I saw that in her mind when I was there, but I don't know how to *do* it."

"That's supposed to be *private*, Ro," Chloe shot over.

Kevin pushed the alien's floating form gently away from the cockpit space.

"Come on," he said. "You still need to show me how to get the shield working."

"Here," Ro said, pointing. "This relay should control it. We need to open this panel."

Kevin braced his feet against the wall, pulling until he felt the panel give way. There were things inside that looked like wires, and other things that looked more grown than made. Points on the relay were blackened and withered, as if burnt by fire.

"We need to reroute it," Ro said, pressing long fingers to a couple of points in the relay. "Yes, I am not Pure anymore, but I know how to do this. *I* know."

There was a glow as some kind of connection came back into place, and Kevin found himself tumbling the short distance to the floor, landing with a bump.

"The shield is back in place," Ro said.

"So we're protected?" Kevin asked, hoping it would be enough to shield them from everything from the energy weapons of the planet's inhabitants to the Hive's world-shattering blast. Even as he said it, he knew the answer. The first blast had ripped through them like it was nothing.

"The shield keeps air in, allows control of gravity, and stops minor impacts, no more," Ro said.

That, Kevin suspected, was going to be a problem, *especially* since the view out of the window showed the ship that had shot at them coming around for another pass.

"We're limping in space," Chloe said, pulling at the joystick. "This thing is moving slower than the boat did after the storm."

Kevin suspected that it was going a lot faster than that, but if they couldn't maneuver properly, then it didn't really make a difference. They were just sitting ducks for the aliens who were even now lining up to fire at them again. Kevin almost thought of them as his enemies, but they *weren't*, they were the opposite of enemies. They just thought that he and the others were something that they weren't.

Maybe they should let them know the truth, then.

"Is the radio working?" Kevin asked.

Chloe shrugged. "I don't know, let me try. Testing, testing, can anybody hear us?"

"Who is this?" a voice called over the radio, and Kevin recognized the language of the aliens who had tried to warn them even as his mind translated it automatically.

"Wow," Chloe said. "I can understand them."

"It is probably an effect of the symbiont," Ro said, which just made Kevin look uncomfortably at the thing covering Chloe's arm. He hated that the people around him kept being changed or hurt. He hated that he'd told them to take her away and do it.

"Who is this?" the voice repeated.

"This is Kevin McKenzie," Kevin said into the radio. "I have my friend Chloe here, and an alien named Ro who used to be one of the Hive. Um… please don't shoot us down."

The radio crackled. "Kevin McKenzie? The human who tried to trick us? Who has helped to destroy this world?"

135

"Um…" Kevin said, not sure what kind of answer there *could* be to that. It felt as though anything he said right then would mean trouble for them all.

"That's right," Chloe said into the radio, while he was still trying to think of what to say. "They made him into one of them. They made him do… all kinds of stuff. But we got him back. We broke out."

Through the window, Kevin could still see the ship approaching, hanging there in front of them. Its weapons glowed with the prospect of the blast to come.

"Impossible," the voice said. "Those taken by the Hive do not break free of it. There is no way to beat the whole Hive."

"There *is*," Kevin insisted. "I saw it while I was one of them. I know their weaknesses."

There was the briefest of pauses from the radio, presumably as whoever was on it conferred with a superior.

"The risk is too great," the voice there said. "We have never heard of anyone breaking free from the Hive, and you have already tried to trick us. We believe that this is just some attempt to get close to us. We are sorry, but you must be stopped."

"Wait!" Kevin shouted. "You need to listen to us. The Hive is going to try to destroy your world."

"We know," the voice said, "and we cannot evacuate because you are targeting our escape ships."

Kevin winced at the reminder of that. He'd been the one to suggest it, and to find the ships for the Hive. He looked over to Ro.

"Are you still blocking the Hive?" he asked.

Ro shook his head. "There has been too much happening to maintain concentration, but I could try to reestablish the connection."

"Do it," Kevin said.

He saw Ro sink into the trance of concentration that he'd held before. "I have it."

"Listen to me," Kevin said. "The alien who used to be a part of the Hive is doing his best to confuse the Hive. It won't last long, but it should give your ships some time to get away."

"Do you think we're going to listen to you?" the voice at the other end of the line demanded. "After all you've done? After all the people who are dead because of you?"

Kevin swallowed at the thought of that. He knew the things that he'd done as a part of the Hive.

"They didn't give Kevin any *choice*," Chloe snapped. "And now, you don't have any choice either. They're going to blow your world up; you can either get your people off it or sit there and argue with us."

This time, the pause seemed to stretch out for several seconds, and in those seconds, Kevin found himself staring at the ship coming toward them. It still raced forward, its weapons still charged to deliver the killing blow. What would it be like if it did fire? Would it be instant for them this time, vaporized in a wash of energy? Would they be sucked out into space?

Then the ship raced past, lost to view in an instant, and Kevin saw more ships rising up from the planet's surface, rising like spores from a mushroom, or the dying gasp from a drowning man. They were the last life on the planet.

Some found themselves shot down, caught out by Hive ships that were in the right place to intercept them. More got through, though, and Kevin could see the Hive's vessels pulling back, moving into the world ship, seeking cover against what was going to come. The world ship hung there, white hot and menacing, charged with power, ready to fire.

It fired.

The beam lanced out from the world ship to the planet below in an instant, in a beam of radiance that looked like a pencil-thin line to Kevin, but must really have been far wider, because he'd seen the scale of the opening that they'd made in the world ship to let it fire through. That line of energy struck down at the world below and Kevin watched in horror as it did its work.

"When they fire, the atmosphere boils off first," Ro said, as a rim of red appeared around the planet, as if the air itself there were on fire. To Kevin, it made the whole thing look like a comet on a scale a hundred, a thousand times bigger. "They usually like to strip it of useful gases before they do it, because of that."

"Don't," Chloe said.

"Then the seas boil, and the land burns," Ro said, as Kevin saw what looked like swirling hurricanes traveling over the surface, arching up into space because there was no atmosphere to hold them in. "Again, the Hive would normally drain such liquids, but—"

"Don't *tell* us what's happening," Chloe said. "It's horrible enough without you telling us."

Kevin had to agree that it was. The world below had been a place of blue and green, a vibrant, living place. Now, instead, it ran with waves of red and orange, burning, then charring, pressures building up within it, the energy breaking it apart. He saw fissures opening on the surface as the energy beam lanced inside, great gouts of volcanic magma flaring up the way the seas had. The world seemed to throb from within like a heart beating too fast, pushed to its limits, the energy poured into it too much for whatever liquid metals lay at its core…

"Prepare yourselves," Ro said, taking a grip on the pilot's console. Kevin did the same.

Then the world below exploded.

It did it in a blaze of light so bright that for a moment or two, Kevin couldn't see anything. He squeezed his eyes shut, and the spot where the world had been seemed to be burned onto the inside of his eyelids, caught in the instant of splintering into a hundred thousand fragments.

The ship rolled and shook as rocks battered it, the impacts banging and rattling as they struck against it. Without the shields that they'd managed to get in place, Kevin was certain that they would have been torn into pieces. As it was, they bounced around on a tide of fragments, the energy of the explosion carrying them along like a boat being borne by a tidal wave. It felt like being on a rollercoaster, and it took all the strength Kevin had to cling onto the pilot's console. He saw Ro flung across the ship by the force of it, slumping against the far wall, while Chloe's face was white as she hung onto the ship's joystick.

The force seemed to last forever, and when it passed, it took several seconds for Kevin's brain to register that it had. He groaned and managed to struggle up from the floor, only realizing as he did so that he'd fallen. Ro and Chloe were groaning too, and that was probably a good thing in its way, because at least it meant that they were both alive to do it.

"What…" Kevin managed. He looked around, seeing rock after rock beyond the confines of the ship, drifting in a field of asteroids, some small, some the size of a car, some the size of a city or a small country. They drifted and jolted, some smashing into one another and fracturing apart.

There was no sign of the world ship.

"They've pulled back," Ro said. He sounded confused. "But the Hive does not work like that. The Hive takes the resources. It collects all that it can. It does not *waste*."

"Not here," Chloe said. "Here, they just wanted to destroy everything."

"They wanted to make an example," Kevin said. He'd been a member of the Hive long enough to understand that. "They wanted to make it clear that this wasn't just about taking what they could. They'll be back, though."

138

Once they were sure that they'd made their point, once the ashes had cooled, they would come for what they could. Ro was right: the Hive didn't waste.

"We'll need to get out of here before then," Kevin said. "Where are we?"

Ro looked at some of the instruments on the pilot's console. "We've been pushed further out by the force of the blast into the system. Things will be unstable here, with the gravitational effect of the planet gone."

"Then we should find a way to go," Kevin said. "We need to work out a way back."

"How?" Ro said. "This is a small craft, designed to dart to a world and fight, not travel across the galaxy."

"It's worse than that," Chloe said, jerking at the joystick. Kevin looked up, expecting to see the sky outside swinging around. Instead, nothing happened.

They were stuck there. They had no power, no food, and nowhere to go even if they had all of it.

They were stranded.

CHAPTER TWENTY ONE

Luna watched in horror as the aliens closed in. There were so many of them, too many of them. They were everywhere that she could see, advancing toward the UCLA campus, the sheer unbroken line of them adding to the horror of it. Beside her, Bobby started barking, as if sounding the alarm, but Luna could already see how bad things were.

"Get the crystals and the meteorite," she yelled over to Ignatius. She looked around for anything that she could carry them with, running down to the first floor and into a reception space. She found a couple of plastic boxes there, filled with files. She tipped them out and ran back upstairs with them.

The sounds of battle surrounded her all at once, guns sounding outside, and booms as energy blasts hit the university buildings, sounding in cascades of stone and concrete. Luna looked out of the window to see the fighting starting down below, the Survivors and the others firing guns, spreading the vapor from their few vapor weapons, fighting hand to hand with controlled who weren't even trying to convert them, just striking out trying to kill them. The aliens had learned quickly, or perhaps they just didn't care about making more of the controlled now.

"Down!" Ignatius yelled behind her, and Luna saw the flicker of an energy blast approaching.

She threw herself flat, dragging Bobby with her, and a shower of brickwork flew overhead as the blast hit, cracking casings and shattering glass, Luna felt something scrape across her back, pain flaring, and for a moment she just wanted to lie there until the ringing in her ears went away. Then Bobby licked her face, and Luna realized that she had to get up again.

She scrambled toward the spot where the crystals sat, and where she'd been disappointed with how they looked before, now Luna stared at them. They *glowed*, with a blue light that seemed to fill the space around them.

"They're reacting to the energy of the blast," Ignatius said, struggling to his feet a lot more slowly than Luna had.

The glow faded from the crystals slowly, and they were a dull blue-gray again. Ignatius picked them up, putting them in the plastic boxes as Luna held them out. The meteorite was heavy enough that Luna barely managed to hold it.

"All right," Ignatius said. "We have what we came here for. Now, can we get out of here before we're all killed?"

Luna hoped so. "Come on," she said. "We'll find a way back to the bus."

When she looked out of another of the museum's windows, though, it seemed obvious that things wouldn't be that easy. The plaza in front of the museum was awash with fighting now, and since the controlled looked almost exactly like the people who had been freed from the aliens' control, it was almost impossible to tell the difference from that height. The Survivors who had taken the vapor guns continued to spray people almost at random, and some fell as the vaccine did its work, but the most the ones with real guns could do was fire at anyone who started to attack them, and by then, it seemed to Luna as though it would already be too late.

"I don't think we're getting out until the battle's won," she said. "If we tried to escape now, we would lose half of our people trying."

"If we can get away with a way to win this, then maybe—"

"Don't say it," Luna snapped back at him. "I waited for *you* at the base. We're not abandoning people."

Besides, even if Luna had wanted to, she suspected that there would have been no way to do it. The controlled blocked the exits to the plaza now, while the stranger, alien things stalked into it, striking out with limbs that were weapons in themselves. One went down, brought down by a barrage of shots from the Survivors, but there were more.

"We need to get down there," Luna said. "We need to help."

"And *how* do we help?" Ignatius asked.

Luna didn't have an answer to that. Other people had the vapor guns, and Luna didn't even have their makeshift vapor grenades. Even so, she felt as though she had to do *something*. She couldn't just leave the others to do all of the fighting, and she still at least had a dart gun.

"Wait here," she said to Ignatius.

"Where would I go?" he countered, gesturing to the chaos outside.

"Just… make sure you're here when I get back," Luna said. "I need to check on the others."

She ran downstairs with Bobby by her side, plunging down into the chaos. It was instant. Around her, there were people fighting everywhere she looked, some with the dead white pupils of the controlled, some fighting back noisily, shouting to one another as they did it.

141

"Keep shouting!" Luna said, realizing that it was one thing they could do that the controlled couldn't. "If you're saying something, we can tell that you're not one of them!"

She wasn't sure how many of them heard her, but some did, and they started doing all kinds of things. Some shouted encouragement to one another, some yelled battle cries of their own invention, some sang, only adding to the cacophony of the battle.

Luna saw Leon and Barnaby in the midst of the battle, fighting with controlled after controlled. Barnaby had one of the vapor guns and was spraying it all around, keeping them at bay. Leon was striking out with a machete in one hand and a gun in the other, mostly trying to keep them back from Barnaby long enough for him to change more of them back into people.

Luna started to fight her way across to them, pushing people out of the way, ducking under a pair of grabbing arms and then darting forward past a thing that was swiping out with claws as long as daggers. Another of the controlled jumped at her, and Barnaby leapt to meet it, snapping and snarling, knocking it back with both paws before returning to Luna's side.

She pushed her way through to Leon, lifting her dart gun and bringing down one of the controlled who was moving in from his side.

"We've found it!" she yelled over the noise of the battle. "We've got the substance. We can get out of here!"

She knew that wasn't a real option, but she felt as though she had to say it, just in case there *was* some way out of there that she hadn't seen.

"There are too many of them," Leon said. "There's no way out."

"Then we have to win this," Luna said. She loaded another dart into the dart gun and shot another of the controlled.

Then she saw one of the alien things heading toward them, stalking forward on legs whose knees bent the wrong way, and which had scales that shimmered like an oil slick. It bared crocodilian teeth and roared, swiping people out of its way as it tried to get to them.

Luna loaded one dart after another, firing at it without stopping. A dart plunged into a space between some of the softer scales, then another, pumping the sedative into the beast. It kept coming forward, barely slowed, but Luna kept firing and firing. For a step or two, it didn't seem to make any difference, but then, finally, the alien thing stood there and gave another cry, sounding mournful and bereft, then toppled over like some great scaly tree.

"We got one!" Luna yelled out, punching her fist in the air.

Then she saw a dozen other creatures just like the first coming into the edge of the plaza, smashing into the people there.

"We won the last fight," Luna said, trying to convince herself as much as Leon or Barnaby.

"We're losing this one," Leon replied, shooting at another of the alien things as it came closer. The bullet struck it, but it kept coming, pausing to swing its claws around to rip through a couple more of their people.

People were dying everywhere Luna looked. The controlled were faster and stronger than the humans, and the alien things were even more dangerous than that. They tore into the Survivors, throwing aside the people who had been changed back from being controlled like they were rag dolls.

Amidst the chaos of it all, Luna saw Cub leap forward, hacking with a blade as long as his forearm, slicing into a gap in one of the creatures' armor. He plunged the weapon deep then sprang away, riding the momentum of an arm sweep that tried to send him flying. Luna heard the creature howl and then fall as another dozen people struck at it.

She kept her eyes on Cub. He struck out at one of the controlled and then another, with the kind of confidence that came from years of fighting, and the kind of recklessness that made Luna's heart tighten in her chest to see it.

Then she saw him stiffen and stop, far too still against the rest of the fight. He turned, and Luna could have sworn that he was looking straight at her, standing and just staring against the background of the violence.

"No," Luna whispered. "Please no…"

Her heart all but broke in two as Cub turned back to the fight, moving with the speed of the controlled, his long knife cutting into first one of the Survivors, then another.

"No!" Luna yelled, but it didn't matter what she yelled, didn't matter how much she wanted to run down there and make this stop. Cub was already changed, already one of them, already back to being nothing more than a puppet of the aliens.

"No, this can't happen," Luna said. "I can't… first my parents, then Kevin and Chloe, now Cub, and soon…"

Soon it would be her. Luna could feel the pressure of it inside her, wanting to rise up, striving to take over every second that she didn't push it back down. Soon it would be too much, and maybe it would even be *better* like that. Maybe it would be better not to have to think, not to have to feel, not to have to hurt…

143

An explosion came, and a wall collapsed, and it threw her against Bobby. Both of them lay there, trapped, the controlled closing in, and Luna knew they were finished.

She looked at Bobby, tears in her eyes.

"You're really soft," she told him. "I could just lie here on you and sleep and not wake up."

The trouble was, that was exactly what was going to happen. She would be one of them, and then she would either be lost out in the world, or she would be killed, or she would lose herself so completely that there was no coming back. There was nothing she could do about it.

Maybe it was better to lie there and close her eyes.

She turned to her dog one last time.

"I love you, Bobby."

CHAPTER TWENTY TWO

Kevin had known, from the moment the doctor told him, that he was going to die, but he hadn't thought that it would be like this. The spaceship hung dead in space, in spite of Chloe's attempts to press buttons, and her occasional kicks at the side of the pilot's console. Ro sat on the floor, staring in silence.

"I am starting to think that emotions are not always a good thing," he said. "Before them, I would not fear death. I would not feel so alone."

"You're not alone," Kevin said. "We're here."

"And we're stuck here," Chloe said from the pilot's seat as she brought her hand down on the controls, hard. "I can't get us anywhere."

She had the familiar note in her voice that said that she was on the edge of panic, and for once, Kevin couldn't blame her. Even so, he went over to her and put a hand on her shoulder.

"I know you feel trapped," Kevin said. "I do too, but I'm here. Whatever happens, I'm here."

Chloe managed a brief smile. "I guess if I'm going to die with anyone, I'd like it to be with you."

"I'd rather you didn't have to die with anyone," Kevin said.

"Yeah," Chloe agreed. Her hand closed over his. "I don't want to die, Kevin."

Kevin realized that he didn't want to either. He'd come to terms, kind of, with the idea that he was dying from a disease that he couldn't control, because it didn't look as though there was anything else he could do about it. This was something different, though. This cut away even the little time that he'd thought he'd had.

"I know," Kevin said. "I wish…"

He wished all kinds of things: that he hadn't tried to stop the Hive with a virus that hadn't worked. That it hadn't meant he and Chloe had been taken to the world ship. That he'd been able to stop the Hive from making him a part of it. That he hadn't hurt Chloe. That he hadn't been a part of destroying the world below.

There was no world there now, just a field of asteroids beyond the ship that bumped and bounced from one another like balls in some gigantic game. Ro had seemed horrified before that the Hive had left without taking any of it, and Kevin guessed that he could see that. If they were going to destroy a world to steal every resource it had, that was evil enough, but to do it and just abandon what they had destroyed? There wasn't even any reason to it then. It was just cruelty for its own sake.

Mostly, though, he just found himself thinking about the people who must have been on the planet when it burned.

"How many people do you think were down there?" he asked.

"It is impossible to know," Ro said. "The shields blocked any attempt to scan them, and even then, the Hive would not have found everyone. Not many, I would guess. A few tens of thousands."

"Tens of thousands," Kevin repeated, thinking of the way he'd helped to let the Hive in. Tens of thousands of alien creatures could be dead because of him.

"It is hard to be sure," Ro said. "This was a place of refuge rather than their home world, so I doubt that their entire population would be there, and there are only so many it is possible to hide, but I suppose that theoretically, as many as a million might—"

"You aren't helping, Ro," Chloe said. "Kevin, this isn't your *fault*. You didn't have a *choice*."

"I still did it though," Kevin said. "When it happened, it was still my voice giving the orders, my brain making the decisions."

"Not your brain, the Hive," Ro said.

Kevin shook his head. "You know what it's like as well as I do," he said. "It's still your brain in there. Just your brain without any of the emotions."

"Without compassion," Chloe said. "Without a conscience. They took those things away. You can't blame yourself for not having them."

Kevin tried, but it was impossible not to look at the vast field of asteroids and feel guilt. It was impossible not to imagine the screams of people as they died in a disaster that he had helped to make. Before all this, he had tried never to hurt anyone. He'd gotten in only a few fights, and most of those had been because he'd been backing Luna up. Now, he might have been responsible for a million deaths... it was too much. It was too *many*.

"Some people will have gotten out," Chloe said, standing up to put a hand on his shoulder.

"A million?" Kevin asked, thinking of the transport ships he'd helped to target.

"More people than would have escaped if you hadn't warned them, and Ro hadn't distracted the Hive," Chloe said. "As soon as you were yourself again, you tried to help. You *did* help."

146

"Just not enough," Kevin said. "Not enough to save all those people, and not enough to save you."

"I don't need saving," Chloe said, with a defiant look.

"We all do," Kevin replied. "We're sitting here in space, and if we sit here long enough, we'll starve, or we'll crash into an asteroid."

Kevin wasn't sure which he would prefer. The first option gave them more time, but more time to do what? Hang in space and feel guilty? The second option would at least be quick, but Kevin couldn't bring himself to wish for it. A part of him still wanted to keep going, because as long as they were still alive, there was still hope, there was—

"I think that there is a problem," Ro said, in a concerned tone.

Kevin looked over to see him staring down at the pilot's console. A red light was starting to blink there.

"What does it mean?" Chloe demanded, the fear in her voice easy to hear.

"It's probably nothing," Kevin said, trying to reassure her automatically, even while he could feel his own fear building, making his throat feel tight, his breath coming shorter, the air feeling thin around them.

"It is the oxygen sensor," Ro said. "I'm sorry, I feel that was a bad thing to say."

"We're losing oxygen?" Kevin said. Did that mean that the way he felt right then was real? He felt as though the room was closing in, the air pressing in on him.

"I thought we got the shield back up," Chloe said.

"It may not be perfect, and with the damage to the ship..." Ro said.

"So we're all going to die?" Chloe said, and Kevin could hear the panic building in her voice.

"We were all going to die anyway," Ro said. "This way, we are merely going to die in a few minutes, rather than—"

"It's really *not helping*, Ro!" Chloe snapped, moving away from the pilot's seat and going to huddle into a ball next to the wall.

Kevin went to sit down next to her. He held onto her, not knowing what else to do. He couldn't promise that things would be all right, because they wouldn't. He couldn't tell her that he would make any of it better. All he could do was be there, and maybe, at a time like this, that was enough.

He sat there, holding onto Chloe, not saying anything because there was nothing he could say that he wasn't already showing her just by being there. He felt the warmth of her huddled close to him, but he also felt the way the air was getting thinner, felt the way that each breath seemed to bring a little less life with it than the last.

"How long do you think we have?" Chloe asked.

"I don't know," Kevin said. He was already starting to feel a little faint from the lack of air. "I just... if I have to die with someone, I'm glad it's you."

"I'd rather be on a beach somewhere," Chloe said.

"Yeah, me too."

He sat with her silently after that, feeling his breaths come shorter and shorter as the oxygen ran out.

He could see the room growing darker and darker, the edges of his vision closing in around him.

Chloe was still beside him, her breathing so shallow that Kevin could barely feel or hear it.

Ro hadn't said anything for a while now.

Blackness closed in on Kevin.

This it, he knew.

This is how it ends.

NOW AVAILABLE!

RETURN
(The Invasion Chronicles—Book Four)

"TRANSMISSION is riveting, unexpected, and firmly rooted in strong psychological profiles backed with thriller and sci-fi elements: what more could readers wish for? (Just the quick publication of Book Two, Arrival.)"
--Midwest Book Review

From #1 worldwide bestselling fantasy author Morgan Rice comes book #3 in a long-anticipated science fiction series. With planet Earth destroyed, what will become of 13 year old Kevin and Chloe in the mother ship?

Will the aliens enslave them? What do they want? Is there any hope of escape?

And will Kevin and Chloe ever return to Earth again?

"Action-packed …. Rice's writing is solid and the premise intriguing."
–Publishers Weekly, re A Quest of Heroes

"A superior fantasy… A recommended winner for any who enjoy epic fantasy writing fueled by powerful, believable young adult protagonists."
–Midwest Book Review, re Rise of the Dragons

"An action packed fantasy sure to please fans of Morgan Rice's previous novels, along with fans of works such as THE INHERITANCE CYCLE by Christopher Paolini…. Fans of Young Adult Fiction will devour this latest work by Rice and beg for more."
–The Wanderer, A Literary Journal (regarding Rise of the Dragons)

Book #4 in the series will be available soon.

Also available are Morgan Rice's many series in the fantasy genre, including A QUEST OF HEROES (BOOK #1 IN THE SORCERER'S RING), a free download with over 1,300 five star reviews!

Books by Morgan Rice

THE INVASION CHRONICLES
TRANSMISSION (Book #1)
ARRIVAL (Book #2)
ASCENT (Book #3)
RETURN (Book #4)

THE WAY OF STEEL
ONLY THE WORTHY (Book #1)

A THRONE FOR SISTERS
A THRONE FOR SISTERS (Book #1)
A COURT FOR THIEVES (Book #2)
A SONG FOR ORPHANS (Book #3)
A DIRGE FOR PRINCES (Book #4)
A JEWEL FOR ROYALS (BOOK #5)
A KISS FOR QUEENS (BOOK #6)
A CROWN FOR ASSASSINS (Book #7)
A CLASP FOR HEIRS (Book #8)

OF CROWNS AND GLORY
SLAVE, WARRIOR, QUEEN (Book #1)
ROGUE, PRISONER, PRINCESS (Book #2)
KNIGHT, HEIR, PRINCE (Book #3)
REBEL, PAWN, KING (Book #4)
SOLDIER, BROTHER, SORCERER (Book #5)
HERO, TRAITOR, DAUGHTER (Book #6)
RULER, RIVAL, EXILE (Book #7)
VICTOR, VANQUISHED, SON (Book #8)

KINGS AND SORCERERS
RISE OF THE DRAGONS (Book #1)
RISE OF THE VALIANT (Book #2)
THE WEIGHT OF HONOR (Book #3)
A FORGE OF VALOR (Book #4)
A REALM OF SHADOWS (Book #5)
NIGHT OF THE BOLD (Book #6)

THE SORCERER'S RING
A QUEST OF HEROES (Book #1)

A MARCH OF KINGS (Book #2)
A FATE OF DRAGONS (Book #3)
A CRY OF HONOR (Book #4)
A VOW OF GLORY (Book #5)
A CHARGE OF VALOR (Book #6)
A RITE OF SWORDS (Book #7)
A GRANT OF ARMS (Book #8)
A SKY OF SPELLS (Book #9)
A SEA OF SHIELDS (Book #10)
A REIGN OF STEEL (Book #11)
A LAND OF FIRE (Book #12)
A RULE OF QUEENS (Book #13)
AN OATH OF BROTHERS (Book #14)
A DREAM OF MORTALS (Book #15)
A JOUST OF KNIGHTS (Book #16)
THE GIFT OF BATTLE (Book #17)

THE SURVIVAL TRILOGY
ARENA ONE: SLAVERSUNNERS (Book #1)
ARENA TWO (Book #2)
ARENA THREE (Book #3)

VAMPIRE, FALLEN
BEFORE DAWN (Book #1)

THE VAMPIRE JOURNALS
TURNED (Book #1)
LOVED (Book #2)
BETRAYED (Book #3)
DESTINED (Book #4)
DESIRED (Book #5)
BETROTHED (Book #6)
VOWED (Book #7)
FOUND (Book #8)
RESURRECTED (Book #9)
CRAVED (Book #10)
FATED (Book #11)
OBSESSED (Book #12)

About Morgan Rice

Morgan Rice is the #1 bestselling and USA Today bestselling author of the epic fantasy series THE SORCERER'S RING, comprising seventeen books; of the #1 bestselling series THE VAMPIRE JOURNALS, comprising twelve books; of the #1 bestselling series THE SURVIVAL TRILOGY, a post-apocalyptic thriller comprising three books; of the epic fantasy series KINGS AND SORCERERS, comprising six books; of the epic fantasy series OF CROWNS AND GLORY, comprising eight books; of the epic fantasy series A THRONE FOR SISTERS, comprising eight books (and counting); and of the new science fiction series THE INVASION CHRONICLES, comprising four books. Morgan's books are available in audio and print editions, and translations are available in over 25 languages.

Morgan loves to hear from you, so please feel free to visit www.morganricebooks.com to join the email list, receive a free book, receive free giveaways, download the free app, get the latest exclusive news, connect on Facebook and Twitter, and stay in touch!

Made in the USA
Coppell, TX
24 March 2020